Midnight Showdown

Rob Hill

A Black Horse Western

ROBERT HALE · LONDON

© Rob Hill 2013
First published in Great Britain 2013

ISBN 978-0-7198-0702-2

Robert Hale Limited
Clerkenwell House
Clerkenwell Green
London EC1R 0HT

www.halebooks.com

Typeset by
Derek Doyle & Associates, Shaw Heath
Printed and bound in Great Britain by
CPI Antony Rowe, Chippenham and Eastbourne

For Val and Joss

1

The engine's iron wheels shrieked against the rails, couplings crashed together and steam exploded; the train juddered to a halt. The evening sky was red with bloody fire, stark silhouettes of the leafless trees stood guard against the sunset and snow carpeted the ground. It was the middle of nowhere.

Men hauled open the doors of the trucks and set up the ramps for the horses; their breath hung in front of their faces. The engine pounded impatiently as the driver kept up a head of steam. With the horses unloaded, the men checked their weapons and mounted up. There was no need to talk: they knew what they had to do.

Right on cue, a rider wearing farm clothes emerged from the woodland a hundred yards away and beckoned them to follow. Stony-faced, the men pulled their jackets tight against the cold, wound their scarves round their faces and pulled their hats down. As they urged their horses forward, the dying light glinted on the Pinkerton National Detective Agency badges pinned to their coats.

The riders followed the track into the woods in single file. Apart from the hoots of faraway owls, the evening was silent. Their guide turned in his saddle.

'Making history tonight, boys.'

No one answered.

They reached the James farmhouse at midnight. It was a single-storey wooden building fronted by a wide porch. Moonlight lit the snow-covered roof, the broken fences and the empty yard. A line of smoke from a dying fire rose from the stone chimney; there were no lights.

'We should check the barn.' Clem pulled down the scarf which covered his mouth and turned to Jackson, the officer in charge. 'If their horses are here, then they are.'

Clement Greenwood had joined the agency during the war. Jackson liked him. In his latest report he described Clem as 'tough, courageous and too high-minded for his own good'.

'Daren't make a sound.' As officer in charge Jackson's greatest fear was losing another man. 'You know what happened to the last fella.'

They all knew. The last Pinkerton to have tracked down Frank and Jesse turned up dead with a note pinned to his jacket which read: *The same to all agents.*

'The family's in there,' Clem insisted. 'We got to be sure.'

'Can't risk it.' Jackson glared at him. 'We've got moonlight. We can see who runs out.'

He nodded to the other agents. Still mounted up, they spread out along the line of trees facing the house.

One man climbed down and unlaced his saddle-bags. He unpacked cotton wads, a bottle of turpentine and a heavy steel ball. Jackson nodded.

'When you're ready.'

The agents facing the house drew their Colts. The man walked his horse down the side of the house, keeping close to the line of trees.

'We should check the barn,' Clem said again. 'If the place goes up we'll have blood on our hands.'

'I've told you,' Jackson snapped. 'We can't risk it. My priority is to make sure all my agents stay alive.'

Tiny snowflakes began to drift down in the moon-light. They sparkled in the manes of the horses and settled on the hats of the men. The agent beside the house uncorked the bottle and poured liquid over a wad of cotton. He struck a flint and orange fire flared in the darkness. Shadows of the trees lurched on the snow. Flame arced through the darkness as the agent threw the burning wad towards the window. It fell short, hissed and spluttered out on the ground.

Jackson waved furiously at him to try again.

The man dismounted, crept up to the side of the house and, when he was under the window, reached up and smashed the glass. Then he lit a second wad. As the ball of flame reared in his hand he flung it inside.

Jackson gestured to him to keep going; the agent threw in a second flare. Then there was uproar. A

9

woman screamed; a man shouted. There were children's terrified voices. It sounded as though furniture was being hurled across the room. The line of agents covered the door with their Colts. The man beside the house flung in a third burning wad. The yelling continued.

Jackson pointed to where smoke billowed up from the chimney.

'They're throwing them in the fireplace,' he snarled. 'This ain't gonna work.'

'There's children in there,' Clem hissed. 'You got to call 'em out.'

Jackson cupped his hands round his mouth.

'Throw in the Greek fire.'

The words echoed across the snowy yard. The line of agents tightened their grips on their reins.

'No,' Clem shouted.

'Now,' Jackson yelled.

The man under the window lit a fuse which trailed from the iron ball in his hand. It fizzed and spat in the darkness. Inside, shouting and crying rocked the house. The agent lobbed the bomb through the window. The casing was crammed with gelignite; when the fuse burned down, the sides shrapnelled apart.

They all heard the thud as the iron ball landed on the floor inside. The shouting stopped for a second. Then the explosion roared. A lightning flash lit the windows. Yellow flame speared up through the chimney.

'No,' Clem yelled again.

He spurred his horse forward across the yard. Jack

shouted at him to stop. Before he reached the house, the door opened and a little girl in a torn nightdress stood there in the moonlight. Smoke billowed behind her. She stepped dazed and barefoot out onto the porch. Clem leapt down off his horse and snatched her up in his arms.

A woman followed the girl out onto the porch. She moved with ghostly steps; her arm hung torn and useless beside her. A man followed her. He held a boy in his arms. They stood there and stared at the line of mounted men.

Then the man registered Clem, who held the girl; he saw the Pinkerton shield pinned to his coat.

'Put her down.' The words tore at his throat. 'You ain't to go near her or any one of us. We're a peaceful family. Just look what you've done.'

Clem gently lowered the girl back down on her feet. She dived to her mother, flung her arms round her waist and buried her head in her skirts.

Ignoring Jackson and the others, Clem strode across the yard to the barn and wrenched open the door. There was a farm cart in there and a lone carthorse in its stall.

'See,' Clem shouted. 'We should have checked.'

Jackson shoved his Colt back into his holster and signalled to the men to follow him back into the woods.

'You're just going to leave 'em like this?' Clem yelled.

'Get out,' the old man yelled. 'You Pinkertons killed my son. You ain't never gonna catch Frank and Jesse.

11

They're too quick for you.'

Horrified, Clem ran over to see. It was true. The boy in his arms was still; his head lolled back and his arms hung down limp. A curved iron shard was bedded in his chest; there was blood round his mouth.

'I tell you one thing.' The man's face twisted with anger. 'When they hear about this, you're all dead men.'

Clem mounted up and followed the others into the trees.

The old man's voice echoed after them.

By the time the column reached the rendezvous Clem had made up his mind.

The train waited for them at the river bridge. Fists of steam punched up into the night. One of the rail hands had opened the door to the truck and laid down ramps ready for the horses. Moonlight scattered diamonds over the snow; above everything, stars decorated the sky.

Clem rode up to Jackson.

'I ain't coming.'

'You're a Pinkerton Agent,' Jackson snapped. 'You'll do what I say.'

'Not any more,' Clem said. 'I resign.'

He tore the tin shield off his coat and held it out.

'I was under cover down here in the war,' Clem continued. 'I saw enough for one lifetime then.'

'What are you talking about?' Jackson said.

'That was an innocent kid. You should have checked the barn.'

'I was acting on good information. We've had a man watching the James place for weeks,' Jackson said. 'Added to that, none of my men got hurt.'

'No more than ten years old,' Clem went on.

The other men had loaded their horses onto the train now.

'Boss.' One of them leaned out of the truck. 'You comin'?'

'You taking this or not?' Clem thrust the steel badge at Jackson.

'You ride up to Chicago and hand it to Mr Pinkerton yourself,' Jackson sneered. 'Ask him whether some backwoods kid brother of Jesse James is worth risking the life of one of his agents for.'

Jackson turned his horse up the ramp.

'You choose to stay round here, fine. That old man is Frank and Jesse's step-pa; he got a real good look at you. When Frank and Jesse hear about this, you're going to be the first one they come after.'

Jackson dismounted at the top of the ramp. Steam burst from under the engine.

'When they find you, you're gonna wish we was with you, that's all I can say.'

Clem shoved the badge in his pocket. The rail hand heaved the ramp up into the truck and pulled himself up after it.

Jackson had one last try. 'You're making a mistake, Clem.'

'The day the Pinks kill a kid is the day I quit,' Clem called. 'That's what I'll tell Allan Pinkerton when I get to Chicago.'

The engine's great iron wheels shifted and began to turn. The truck jerked and the couplings clashed. Steam from the boiler thudded against the sky. Clem knew Jackson was right. If the James brothers were in the county, they would be looking for him by morning. As the train moved out he wheeled his horse towards the woods.

As he rode through the silver landscape faces haunted Clem. Dr Samuel, the wild-eyed old man with his ragged grey beard who had given up doctoring and moved on to the James place with his kids when he married Frank and Jesse's mother; Zerelda, putty, faced and weak with her tattered hand, which would need amputation if she didn't bleed to death first; Sara Louise, Jesse's half-sister, who by some miracle had escaped the Pinkerton firebomb unscathed. Then there was little Archie, with his head lolled back and his eyes closed. And for what? Frank and Jesse weren't even there.

Clem had spent the war under cover for the Pinkertons right here in Missouri. He'd seen some sights. But behind all the barn burnings, roadside atrocities and the casual killings there had been a reason. That reason kept him down here, encouraged him in the face of danger, gave him strength to fight for the Union.

Tonight the Pinkertons had attacked a farmhouse while the parents and children were asleep. And why? So they didn't have to risk warning a couple of outlaw brothers, so they didn't have to risk anything at all.

An image of the piece of shrapnel lodged in the

14

child's chest stayed in front of Clem's eyes. The dead boy's face was as vivid to him as when he had stood there. Clem struggled to push the vision to one side and concentrate on the dark trail ahead. The freezing air seared his cheeks and stung his eyes. Ice crystals in the mane of his horse glittered in the moonlight.

Maybe he had been looking for an excuse to leave the Pinks, Clem thought. After all, he'd joined them in the middle of the war more to get away from home than anything else. A brave young Missouri boy with a deep loathing of all the cruelties of the South was a gift to the Pinkertons; they snapped him up. He'd spent two years under cover, passing information about troop movements, new units and the personalities of Confederate officers back to his contacts, who in turn relayed them to Pinkerton HQ. No one even came close to suspecting that he wasn't the loyal Southern boy he pretended to be.

Clem had first heard the names of Frank and Jesse James during the war. He had been ordered to look into the movements of Quantrill's Raiders, the outfit Frank and Jesse rode with. Savage and unpredictable, the Raiders' attacks were a nightmare for the strategists at Union HQ. What little Clem had been able to discover he had passed on; this included the address of the James farm.

When Clem heard what the local Union commander did with this information it disgusted him even in the shocking context of the war. But it was out of his hands; he was miles away at the time. When old man Samuel wouldn't give up the whereabouts of his stepsons and the rest of Quantrill's boys, the commander had him strung up to one of his own trees and went at him with a horsewhip. Hours later when he was barely alive and still refused to talk, the commander gave up. This was the same man Clem had seen only hours before, holding the bloody body of his dead son.

Along the narrow path, the moon lit deer-tracks in the snow. Crystals of frost were heaped on the lower branches of the trees; snow jacketed the roots. Cold held the air still. The jingle of Clem's horse's bridle was a comforting sound in the darkness.

Twenty miles due east was the farm where Clem grew up. He couldn't quite remember whether he had run away home or his pa had thrown him out. Either way, the place held bad memories for him and he had never been back.

Clem's father was an embittered drunk who trumpeted outdated loyalty to the Southern cause instead of trying to make his run-down scrap of land pay. He had let the farm run back until the work defeated him and poverty made him bitter.

With the last years of the war raging around them, the teenage Clem suggested that there was a better way for them to live than crowing allegiance to a losing side just because they happened to live where they did. His father's fury knew no bounds. Having taken a bullet at Bull Run, and now with his wife gone and his farm failing, the only thing he had left was a deluded belief in a glorious victory for the South. To have this challenged by a son who was too smart for his own good was too much for him. The night Clem left home, his irate father followed him with a shotgun.

In the hour before light broke the sky, the cold deepened. Somewhere up ahead an owl whooed. The surface of the snow was brittle under the horse's tread; the few dead leaves which still clung to the lower branches were crisp with ice. Clem leaned forward to pat the neck of his horse; frost had stiffened his coat.

Even with his jacket tight round him and his scarf binding his face, the cold tightened the muscles of Clem's shoulders and crept into his bones. Each breath made a cloud of crystals through his scarf and before he could draw another, ice formed a sheen on the weave. He had not felt his hands or feet for hours.

After the war, Allen Pinkerton himself had insisted Clem stayed on with the agency. Clem spent the next ten years pursuing lawbreakers all over the Midwest. The Pinks were respected by friend and foe alike; Clem was proud to work for them. But as the organization grew there was talk of a new type of work to run alongside the pursuit of lawbreakers.

The country prospered quickly after the war. Businesses needed to protect their interests and were prepared to pay. They wanted information on potential strikers; they wanted the agency to provide under cover operatives who would identify the leaders amongst the working men.

This didn't sit well with Clem. He had joined the Pinks to fight against slave-owners; now it looked as though he would be asked to take the side of bosses. Then there was tonight's business at the James farm. He couldn't get the image of the dead boy out of his

17

head. Even though he had no idea what the future might hold, Clem had to quit the Pinkertons.

Fat snowflakes fell as Clem headed for his old neighbour's place, a smallholding which bordered the farm where he had grown up. His boyhood friend Johnny Sands farmed it now. Even though he hadn't seen Johnny for years Clem knew he could confide in him. He was the only person he could turn to in the whole of Missouri.

2

Exhausted after the night's long ride and with the cold in possession of his bones, Clem approached the rise. Grey, pre-dawn light pushed across the eastern sky and a line of fire ran along the horizon. He was two miles east of Stoneheart, where the land climbed into a series of rolling hills and fell into wooded valleys. The farmers here cleared patches of woodland for their houses and in summer kept their sheep and cattle on the high land where the good grazing was. In winter, they brought their livestock down and kept them in pens near their houses to protect them from the weather and the wolves.

This was where Clem had grown up. His father's farm was west of here and the Sands place was the other side of the rise. Clem knew every hill, every stream, every tree and every rock. He had spent his childhood working on the farm and had regularly driven hogs over this hilltop to sell them at the market in town.

Clem's early childhood had been happy. He was

innocent of the fact that his father only just scratched a living and rarely got a good price for his livestock. To Clem, it was normal to be hungry and to spend the summer without shoes. He learned that his mother lost her sense of humour whenever his father was around and that it was best to make himself scarce when he saw his pa reach for the bottle of rye. But there were chores to do and traps to set; if he had any free time he would visit his friend Johnny Sands, who was exactly his age, on the farm in the neighbouring valley.

One day, during the summer when Clem was ten, a drifter walked into the yard and asked for work. Clem couldn't remember clearly what the man looked like except that his clothes were ragged, he never raised his voice and never caught your eye. He carried a bedroll on his back and Clem remembered thinking he must have walked a long way because his shoes were broken and worn through. Clem's father set him to work building hen houses out of scrap wood while he sat in the kitchen and watched him through the window with the bottle of rye on the table.

A few days later, everything changed.

As Clem walked down the hill one evening after a day watching the sheep, he heard a disturbance in the yard. He could hear his father shouting and the sound of hammering. At least, until he rounded the side of the house, that's what he thought it was.

In the yard, the drifter was lying on the ground by one of the chicken coops he had built. There was a shattered plate and pieces of his mother's cornbread scattered on the ground beside him. The man's arms were raised to cover his head. His father stood over him with an old fence post in his hand. At first Clem thought his pa was waiting to help the man up, ready to hand him the picket to use on the hen house. As Clem stood there, a noise which Clem had never heard before came out of the man's throat; there was blood on his face and clothes. His eyes were open and stared right at Clem. He was dead.

Clem ran into the house. His mother was there, sitting in her chair with her back to the window. There was a mark on her face and she had been crying. She did not seem to hear when Clem screamed at her to know what had happened and what his pa was doing. A thousand questions tore through Clem's head; she wouldn't answer any of them. He couldn't ask his pa; there was an empty bottle on the table.

After that, neither of his parents spoke for days.

A young sheriff called Hackett rode out from Stoneheart. Clem overheard his pa and the sheriff discuss self-defence. His pa described how the man had gone crazy and attacked his wife and then him. He pointed to the mark on his wife's face to prove it. It didn't take Hackett long to make up his mind. He told Clem's father to take the body out into the woods. No more would be said.

A few weeks later Clem's mother took a shotgun out there, put both barrels in her mouth and pulled the trigger.

Five years later, with the war erupting around them and his father vociferous in support of the

Confederacy, Clem slipped away one night to escape his father's drunken rages and join the Union. The recruiting officer passed him on to the Pinkertons.

From the top of the rise, Clem looked down on the Sands place. The snowy hillside fell away in front of him. The woods in the valley gutter had been neatly cleared and the cabin had been positioned so that a stream, which was now a line of ice, flowed though the yard. There was a barn, sheep pens and chicken houses close to the house, all covered with pristine snow. A track led up through the woodland to the Stoneheart road.

Right then a group of riders were heading out from the yard. In a few minutes they would be through the snow-covered woods and out on the road. There were two mounted men and one driving a cart. Clem assumed Johnny Sands was amongst them but he couldn't see from where he was. He made his way over the rise and down the other side of the hill. He would let himself in, build up a fire and wait for his old friend to get back.

Halfway down the slope Clem realized something was wrong. Virgin snow over the sheds and pens meant that they were empty. Had Johnny sold his flock? There were no footprints near the chicken houses either, so no one had been out to feed the hens yet this morning. Only a thin line of smoke rose from the chimney. Didn't Johnny keep the fire in overnight?

Even as a boy Johnny had stood out. He was quick-witted and questioned everything. His mother taught him and Clem to read and write, but Johnny was always way ahead of his friend. It was obvious he was not cut out for farm life. He would rather bury his head in a book than keep the yard tidy.

From childhood, Johnny had loved cards. When his parents were alive he played a hand of gin with them almost every evening. When he ventured into the saloon he quickly mastered poker and euchre; people noticed his convincing wins.

With Johnny it was never a question of money. Cards to him were an exercise in skill and risk, memory and mathematics. If he won, he won; if he lost he laughed and chided himself for not having seized an opportunity or having misjudged a hand. He had a sharp memory and could recall the sequence of a game; afterwards, he would go over it card by card and resolve to do better next time. Win or lose, there was always going to be a next time.

Johnny had the skill to make a good farmer but, with his life thrown into turmoil by the war followed by the deaths of his beloved parents, he didn't have the heart for it. Living alone out here, he did what he had to do to get by and spent all the time he could at a card table in the Stoneheart saloon.

As Clem rode into the yard, morning light cleared the sky; the orange sun was bright through the empty trees. The riders' hoofprints and the tracks of the cart had disturbed the snow and he had been right about the sheep pens: every one was empty. The cabin door was open.

Clem called out:

'Johnny, are you there?'

No answer. He dismounted and looped the reins of his horse round the rail.

'It's Clem.'

His words echoed across the snowy yard.

Clem paused for one last look before he stepped inside. Whoever had brought the wagon out of the barn had left the door swinging on its hinges.

The cabin was a mess. An untidy heap of logs occupied one corner; the wooden bed had been dragged out of the other to be close to the fire. The pieces of a dismantled shotgun, cleaning rags and a can of oil were scattered over the table. A deck of cards littered the floor. A sack of white beans and sack of flour stood on one side of the fireplace. Bunches of onions hung from the ceiling joists. Johnny had pinned old army blankets over the door and windows in an attempt to keep out the cold.

Clem didn't see him at first, but some small noise made him turn. Johnny was hunched over the fire grate, pulling half-burned books out of the embers.

Johnny turned towards him. There was a dark bruise on his cheek and blood round his mouth. A smile spread over his face.

'Hey, stranger.'

His voice was hoarse in his throat.

Johnny lined up the last half-burned book with the others on the floor away from the fire. Thin smoke rose from the pages; the sharp smell of burned paper hung in the air.

Later with a fire spitting, a skillet in the grate and

the cabin full of the smell of beans and onions, Clem sat at the table to put the shotgun back together.

'They said if they came back again, they'd burn the whole place down.' Johnny's eyes sparkled with humour. He shovelled in a mouthful of beans with one hand while holding a ball of snow wrapped in an old rag against his face with the other.

'They're bluffing,' he went on. 'They've said that before.'

Clem sat across the table and watched his old friend. Johnny's optimism was infectious. To start with Clem wanted to grin along with him but then his friend's words showed him where the problem lay.

Johnny leaned forward and spoke quietly.

'All I got to do is raise a stake and get a seat in a game,' he said. 'I'm due for a winning streak. It's gonna happen. Always does.'

He lifted the ice pack away from his cheek.

'You wouldn't make me a loan, would you, Clem?' He grinned his charming grin. 'Pay you back at the end of the game.'

Clem laughed. 'Keep that ice on your face.'

'It wouldn't have to be much,' Johnny continued. 'Just enough to get a seat at the table.'

'You ain't listening to yourself,' Clem snapped. 'How much are these fellas into you for?'

Johnny hesitated. His confident smile melted. He pressed the ice against the bruise.

'Five hundred.' He looked away as if something had suddenly caught his attention outside the window.

Clem waited.

'To the sheriff.'

Johnny inspected the ice pack.

'This needs renewing. I'll just get some fresh snow.'

He pushed his chair away from the table but Clem reached across and grabbed his arm before he could stand. He stared at his old friend.

'Johnny?'

'See you fixed the shotgun,' Johnny said quickly. 'Been meaning to get round to that.'

He pulled away but Clem held him. Johnny turned towards the window again.

'Two fifty to the deputy.'

Johnny looked back at Clem. His face was white; water ran down his cheek where he had been holding the ice.

'Another two fifty to your pa.'

Clem gasped. 'A thousand dollars?'

Johnny turned away again.

'Lady Luck ran out,' he said.

His grin was fainter this time; the singsong in his voice was quieter.

'She'll be back. Law of averages.'

Clem let go of his arm. Unable to stand his friend staring at him, Johnny went outside to renew the ice pack.

Clem looked around. When he had first entered the cabin he saw that it was bare; now he understood that the men had stripped it. Apart from the meagre food supply, the logpile, the bed and the table there was nothing left. If the shotgun hadn't been in pieces, they would have taken that too. They had even driven the wagon out of the barn.

A cloud of icy air followed Johnny back into the cabin. He made pretence of stoking the fire; his embarrassment in front of his old friend was palpable. Clem knew that it wouldn't be long before he made another attempt to ask him for a loan.

'How come you're down this way?' Johnny said. 'I reckoned you'd be behind a desk in Pinkerton's head office by now.'

Clem described the botched attempt to arrest the James brothers. His voice shook as the told the story of what had happened to young Archie.

'Don't lose any sleep over them,' Johnny said. 'Before the war that family was slave-owning scum, just like dozens of others round here.'

Johnny spat into the fire.

'If Zerelda lost a hand and Archie got killed, they had it coming as far as I'm concerned.'

Clem moved his chair nearer the fire.

'Frank and Jesse rode with Quantrill during the war,' Johnny went on. 'Got accustomed to looting and killing; they stole whatever they wanted. War ended ten years ago and they're still doing it.'

'What we did wasn't right,' Clem said. 'We killed a child and maimed a woman. Don't make no odds whether they are related to Jesse James or not.'

Johnny laughed.

'Even Pinkertons can make a mistake,' he said. 'You've always been too high-flown for your own good.'

He knelt on the floor to check on his books. He ran

the palm of his hand over each one to feel the coolness of the bindings.

'Only lost a few pages,' he said.

'You read all those?' Clem said.

'More than once.' Johnny smiled.

'Most I ever read at one time was the description on a Wanted poster,' Clem said.

A sound outside made them turn to the window. A rider headed towards the cabin across the yard, hat pulled down low, blanket wrapped around the shoulders, scarf across the face. The horse was an appaloosa. Even from here, Clem could see it was well cared for.

Clem drew his Colt and waited behind the door with his pistol ready. Johnny stood with his back to the fire. They listened to the rider dismount and tie the horse to the rail.

When the door opened, Clem eased back the hammer of his Colt. The visitor stepped inside and pulled off her hat. A sea of auburn curls tumbled from underneath it. She turned and looked at Clem. A girl faced him. At a glance, she took in his tired, unshaven face, his trail clothes and the Colt in his hand.

'Who were you expecting?' she said fiercely.

Clem slid his gun back into his holster.

'Apologies, ma'am, I didn't know—'

'Ma'am?' The girl laughed delightedly. 'Clem Greenwood, you ain't changed a jot.'

Clem stared.

'Don't you recognize me?'

3

The young woman wore a saddle jacket, a work shirt and men's pants. She stood with her hat in her hand and she was laughing.

'Sarah Lee,' Clem gasped.

Sarah Lee Hackett, the sheriff's daughter. Clem remembered a little bun-faced girl with a basin cut holding her mother's hand one sunny morning outside the store. When he'd caught her eye, she'd buried her head in her mother's skirts.

They both stood there for a second.

'Well,' Sarah Lee said.

'What are you doing here?' Clem said.

'Came out to see how Johnny . . .' She hesitated. 'I was there when those men rode into town.'

Then Clem remembered Sarah Lee outside the town forge. A slim teenager now, she had argued fiercely with the bemused blacksmith whom she accused of rough-handling the pony she had brought in to be shod. He remembered how angry tears had stood in her eyes. She was beautiful. This time shyness made him turn away.

'They threw my books on the fire,' Johnny said. 'Can you believe that?'

'Oh, Johnny,' Sarah Lee said quietly.

She crossed the room and kissed him on the cheek.

'I brought you some things,' she said. 'I heard what the men were saying.'

'They're just hotheads,' Johnny said. 'Makes 'em feel big to sound off. It ain't nothing to worry about.'

He looked from one to the other of them for some kind of agreement.

'You didn't bring any coffee, did you? I had some beans left but they. . . .'

'In my saddle-bag,' Sarah Lee said. 'Fresh bread and biscuits too.'

Johnny picked up a skillet from the grate and went outside to rinse it in the snow.

'They take your coffee pot too?' Clem called after him but the door swung shut and he didn't answer.

Clem knelt by the fire and rearranged the logs.

'Look at this place,' Sarah Lee said.

'Saw a group of them taking his cart away as I came over the rise,' Clem said.

'It's sport for them now,' Sarah Lee went on. 'There ain't nothing left to take.'

'All this is to pay his poker debts?'

'They ride out every now and then and help themselves. In the autumn a whole bunch of them slaughtered his sheep right there in the yard. Held him at gunpoint and made him watch. A few weeks later they came and took his chickens. They wait for him on the saloon porch and make chicken noises whenever he rides into town.'

Sarah Lee looked away. Clem saw the sadness in her face; he heard resignation in her voice.

'Sometimes it seems like the whole town's against him.'

'Doesn't he fight back?' Clem said.

'All he wants is a place at the card table. He doesn't care how much they laugh at him if they give him that.'

'Why don't the sheriff put a stop to it?'

'My pa?' Sarah Lee looked away. 'Johnny owes him a fortune. Your pa too. They reckon if they wait long enough they're going to be able to take the farm. They invite him to sit in with them, give him more and more credit and watch his debts mount up.'

Sarah Lee stared out of the window. Johnny balanced a skillet piled with snow in one hand and had her saddle-bags slung over his shoulder. He left her shotgun strapped to the saddle. He saw her looking and waved cheerfully.

'One day he'll swear he ain't never going to play again,' she said. 'The next he's begging them to deal him in.'

Johnny pushed open the door. He smiled brightly.

'Neighbourly of you to bring coffee,' he said.

Johnny sounded surprised as if he hadn't expected this. From Sarah Lee's faint smile, Clem realized she had done this before.

Johnny set the skillet down on the edge of the grate. Steam hissed where the pan touched the stone.

'You ain't told me what you're doing back here,'

31

Sarah Lee said.

'Quit the Pinkertons,' Clem said simply. 'We staked out the James place up at Kearney. Frank and Jesse weren't there. Archie got killed.'

'Pinkertons did that? How old's Archie now?'

'Nine, maybe. Ten.'

Clem stared into the fire.

Sarah Lee sat down in the chair nearest the fire and looked at him.

'Whole of Clay County will be talking about it in a day or two.'

Clem sat on the floor and leaned back against the chimney breast.

Johnny unpacked the saddle-bags: a loaf, a hunk of bacon, coffee and sugar.

'You ain't popular round here,' Johnny broke in. 'Word got round about what you did in the war. Missouri folks have got long memories.'

The snow had melted in the skillet. Johnny knelt by the hearth and set about brewing coffee in the pan.

'You know what it's like. Everybody is related to everybody. You have a falling-out with a fella fifty miles south of here, you can bet anything you like he's got a cousin somewhere near Stoneheart. When folks heard about you going under cover with the Pinks, they took that as a betrayal.'

Clem's eyes hardened.

'Think I'm worried about what a bunch of old-fangled Missouri farmers think about me?'

'It ain't what they think,' Johnny said. 'It's what they can do.'

'You've got to tread careful,' Sarah Lee said. 'Your pa, my pa and plenty of others round here supported the South. Missouri was on a fault line back then.'

'All this is supposed to be forgotten,' Clem said. 'War's been over for years.'

'Politics is what you read about in the newspapers,' Sarah Lee said. 'Down here, when what happens touches people's families, nobody forgets nothing.'

The coffee boiled over the sides of the pan and hissed on the grate. Johnny snatched the pan back from the flames. He got up to look around for a cup.

'You talking about me and my pa?' Clem said.

'You, your pa, my pa and half the folks in Stoneheart,' Sarah Lee answered.

Clem stared into the fire.

'They must have taken my tin cups,' Johnny said. 'I had two of 'em.'

He got down on all fours and stared under the bed.

Sarah Lee and Clem exchanged a look.

'There's one in the saddle-bag,' Sarah Lee said. 'We can take turns.'

Johnny poured out the oily coffee and the three of them passed the cup between them. None of them wanted to move away from the warmth of the fire.

'Been thinking,' Johnny announced. 'Could get a price for some of that timber out there. There's a couple of big hickories and a white oak.' He glanced at Clem. 'We could take 'em down between us.'

'Folks round here ain't short of timber,' Clem cautioned. 'It's a lot of work if you're thinking of planking it.'

Johnny smiled cheerfully. In his mind the project was already a success. The trees were felled, the planks were measured, cut and stacked in the yard ready for collection.

'Last time I was in town, I heard they're planning to build an extension on to the saloon. They're gonna need timber for that, ain't they? I could take a down payment now and they could settle up on delivery.'

'This is green wood,' Clem said gently. 'They'll buy seasoned pine from St Louis for that.'

Johnny stared into the fire. 'If the timber was cut and right here on the doorstep, they wouldn't have the expense of hauling it. With me giving 'em a good price, I reckon they'd go for it.'

'Check it out first,' Clem said. 'Make a deal before you start work.'

Johnny started to make calculations in his head. The hickories were worth a hundred dollars each at least. He might be able to swing a hundred and fifty. And the oak, well, that must be worth double.

'I got saws in the barn that used to belong to my pa,' Johnny said, 'if they ain't been took. They're rusted now, but they'd clean up fine.'

Suddenly Johnny's enthusiasm for the project was boundless.

'I got oil, whetstones, everything we need. We could sit here by the fire and start right now.'

He beamed at Clem and Sarah Lee, expecting them to share his relish for the idea. They laughed out loud at his earnestness.

Johnny jumped up.

'I'm going out to the barn to find those saws right now.'

He seized a jacket from the peg by the door and flung it round his shoulders. A second later they saw him pass the window.

Clem threw another log on the fire. Sparks exploded up the chimney.

'Is he always like this?'

'Just like a kid, full of wild schemes and craziness. There ain't a harmful bone in his body. You can't help but be fond of him.'

She smiled.

'Trouble is, when he's got cards in his hand he forgets everything else; how much he's won, how much he's lost, whether he's got enough food to make a meal.'

She stared into the fire.

'I've reasoned with him. Some days he'll promise never to play again. Then a few hours later he'll have forgotten what he's said.'

'What about the guys he plays with?'

'I've spoke to them too. My pa says it's a free country. If Johnny chooses to lose his shirt, that's up to him.'

'Ain't he got no other friends?'

'Not now.' Sarah Lee sighed. 'He owed money to half the men in Clay County at one time or another. He paid it all back. But the debts he's got now are too much for anybody.'

'This sack of beans,' Clem looked round the cabin, 'these onions. Did you bring him all this?'

Sarah Lee nodded.

'We had too much for my pa and me. I'll tell you something for nothing,' she went on. 'You may think he's all set on this idea of selling timber but if there was a chance of a poker game, he'd forget the whole thing.'

Dry wood crackled in the fire; orange sparks danced up the chimney.

'What about you?'

'Me?'

Sarah Lee sounded surprised and looked at him as if she didn't know what he meant.

'Not married and settled down?'

She laughed, looked into the fire; she hesitated before she answered.

'Guess the right guy never showed.'

She looked down at the front of her jacket, found some imaginary trail dust and brushed it away.

'Had offers,' she said quietly. 'You know how it is.'

'Not even a sweetheart?'

'Zac Carter is sweet on me, I guess,' Sarah Lee offered shyly. 'He's Pa's deputy; Pa likes him. I go to dances with him sometimes.'

'I remember him,' Clem said. 'Always scrappin'' when he was a kid. You like him?'

'I'm twenty-four years old; there ain't a lot of choice in Stoneheart.'

Sarah Lee scratched at her jacket with her finger-nails; the trail dirt wouldn't come out. Her voice fell to a whisper. 'Pa says I'm an old maid.'

The fire crackled and spat.

'I've got my horses,' Sarah Lee said quickly. 'Appaloosas. Bred 'em myself; I'm training 'em right now. Ain't ready to sell 'em on yet. I will when I find the right buyer. It's got to be someone who'll care for 'em real good.' She looked at Clem. 'Folks round here can be cruel to their horses.'

'Folks everywhere,' Clem said.

'I like coming out here,' Sarah Lee went on. 'Johnny don't think like other people. He's full of ideas and all kinds of dreams. We sit right here and talk and talk. He's got storybooks by Mr Dickens; he reads to me sometimes.'

She laughed at the thought of it.

'What about this deputy?'

'Zac? Sometimes I think being married to him would be like sitting in a jail cell.' Sarah Lee stared out of the window. 'Maybe we would have been sweethearts if you hadn't left.'

Her voice was faint as if she were speaking from far away.

'My pa, the way he was,' Clem said. 'I couldn't stay.'

He felt as if he was excusing himself for abandoning her.

'Their generation are tough people,' she said. 'They're hard on themselves and hard on each other, but they're still kin.'

Clem shook his head.

'Don't make no difference. A lot of what they did was wrong. You know what my pa was like. You know what happened to my ma.'

The door opened and Johnny appeared with a

sunshine grin slapped across his face. He carried a bow saw and a big rusty two-hander under his arm.

'Ain't seen these for a long time,' he declared brightly. 'Found 'em under a hay pile.'

He clattered the saws down on the table. 'Did have some newer ones but they must have been took.'

He strode over to the fire and stood with his back to it.

'We could start with the hickories,' he announced. 'I reckon we could get at least a hundred and fifty for one of 'em.'

'You were going to check to see that you've got a buyer first,' Clem reminded him.

Johnny didn't seem to hear; he produced whet-stones from his pocket.

'Found these in the same place.'

'Gonna need more coffee if we're working on these saws,' Sarah Lee said.

'Sure are.' Johnny grabbed the skillet. 'Nothing like coffee brewing to help you do a job of work.' He laughed out loud at the excitement of starting a new project. As he headed outside to collect more snow, Clem examined the saws. They hadn't been touched for years: flakes of rust broke away under his fingers.

'You realize he won't get a fair price,' Sarah Lee said. 'Even if he finds someone who agrees to buy.'

Clem put the saw down.

'Seen it before,' Sarah Lee said. 'Word goes round and they gang up on him.'

'Who's behind it?'

'All of them. My pa, your pa, everyone he's ever

owed money to.'

She turned to the window. Outside, Johnny was filling the skillet with handfuls of snow.

'He's a sweet guy,' she went on. 'Always thinks the best of people. Even when he knows someone's cheating him, he'll find a reason not to blame them.'

'Ain't many like that,' Clem said.

'That's just it,' Sarah Lee said. 'He ain't like everybody else.'

The door burst open and Johnny was flung bodily inside. He cannoned into the table and brought the saws crashing down on the floor; snow showered everywhere from the skillet he still held in his hand. He ended up face down on the floorboards.

A tall, square-built man stood in the doorway. He was hard-eyed and unshaven; a thin moustache straggled across his top lip. A .45 was strapped to his hip and a deputy's tin star glinted on his jacket. The grey morning light was behind him.

'Zac,' Sarah Lee screamed.

Clem's hand flew to his gun.

'Found some trash in the yard,' Zac boomed. 'So I swept it up.'

He rounded on Sarah Lee.

'You've been told not to come here.' Anger twisted his face. 'Your pa said you'd be here. Sent me to come and fetch you home. What's wrong with you?'

Clem sprang to his feet.

'You need to learn some manners, mister,' he snarled.

Zac seemed to see Clem and the gun in his hand for

the first time.

'Outside,' Clem snapped. 'Right now.'

'I'm deputy sheriff here,' Zac sneered. 'You better put that gun away.'

Sarah Lee ran between them.

'Put the gun away, Clem,' Sarah Lee said. 'I'll go with him. There'll be no shooting.'

'Clem?' Zac said. He squinted at him. 'The Pinkerton?'

'Come on now, Zac,' Sarah Lee said.

Sarah Lee tried to take his arm to ease him out of the door. He shook her off.

'I've heard about you.' Zac's voice scraped his throat. 'You're the traitor, ain't you? Run away from here during the war and sold us out to the Yankees.'

'You were a kid during the war,' Clem said. 'That wasn't your fight.'

Zac took a step back out into the cold morning. Pillows of snow cloud filled the sky. He glared at Clem as if his eyes could burn him up.

'There's folks round here would pay good money to see you dead.'

4

Clem and Johnny stood in the cabin doorway and watched the two riders head into the woods.

'Don't reckon she'll be coming out here no more,' Johnny reflected.

He turned back into the cabin and eyed the provisions on the table.

'You've got to quit the card table,' Clem said.

'Oh, I mean to.' Johnny didn't hesitate. 'Fact is, I'd already made up my mind to do that before you arrived.' He smiled convincingly; he didn't need to be told. 'Got to admit when you're beat, right?'

With an apologetic laugh, Johnny tidied the food Sarah Lee had brought into one corner of the table and set about examining the saws.

'Guess it will take a day to get these cleaned up.'

Clem was surprised at how readily Johnny had agreed with him; maybe Johnny had been doing some thinking. Maybe his plan to make money out of the timber would work after all.

'What kind of fella is this deputy?' he asked.

Johnny scowled. 'All shout and no britches. Reckons if he goes around making a big noise, folks will think he's somebody. Guess he thinks it impresses the sheriff, too.'

'Does it?'

Johnny knelt in front of the grate and stoked the fire. A fistful of sparks exploded up the chimney.

'A dog wants to please its owner, don't he?'

'How does he treat Sarah Lee?'

'Oh, he's sweet on Sarah Lee all right.'

Johnny pretended to examine one of the saws. He picked at the flakes of rust and ran his finger over the blunt teeth.

'Maybe it'll take more than a day.' He looked at Clem. 'To sharpen the saws. Anyhow, I reckon you're right. I should ride into town and get a buyer for the timber before we start.'

Again, Clem was surprised at how quickly Johnny had taken his advice.

'I'll ride along,' Clem said. 'For company.'

'Folks see you with me, I'll never find a buyer,' Johnny said. He shrugged. 'You know how it is round here.'

'Guess I'll head over to see my pa then,' Clem said. 'If you're going to quit poker, maybe I could persuade him to let you off the money you owe him.'

'Your pa?' Johnny scowled again. 'He ain't let nobody off nothing in his whole life.'

'I can try,' Clem said. 'Besides that, I want to tell him that what side someone was on in the war don't matter now.'

'Good luck with that too,' Johnny said.

Outside the air was still. Cold thinned the sunshine; the frozen surface of the fields shone and the light was weak. The branches of the swamp oaks were laced with frost and snow had found its way into the gnarled bark of the hickories. The stream which ran the length of the yard was a sheet of ice.

Startled by the men, a pair of bobwhites hurried along the base of the trees; their white throats and speckled backs made them difficult to see. The rising notes of their alarm call chimed against the snow.

'Won't never go hungry out here if there's quail around,' Clem said.

'They took my box of shells,' Johnny said. 'Only left the shotgun because it was in pieces.'

Clem dug his hands in his jacket pockets, stared hard at the ground and chipped at the snow with the toe of his boot.

'Got money for more?'

'I'll get credit at the store,' Johnny said.

Johnny fetched his horse from the barn. She was an old cow pony, past her best. He led her with a home-made rope bridle.

'No saddle?' Clem said.

'Sheriff took it,' Johnny said. 'Said he was going to give it to your pa as part payment.'

A shadow of hurt crossed Johnny's face. A second later his natural optimism overtook him and he grinned.

'Good thing I hadn't got round to putting that scattergun back together. Never would have got store

43

credit for that.'

He looked at Clem, expecting agreement. Instead Clem leaned back against the wall of the cabin and stared at him hard.

'You've got to stop this.'

'What?' The grin slid from Johnny's face.

'You've got to stop making out all this is some kind of joke,' Clem said. 'Because it ain't.'

'Telling me I ain't allowed to laugh now?' Johnny said.

'These guys are riding roughshod all over you,' Clem went on. 'And you let them.'

Johnny rounded on him. 'You think I invited them out here?'

'I'm just saying,' Clem said, 'you've got to do something about this.'

'I've told you,' Johnny said, 'I've decided. I ain't going near the poker table no more. I'll get a good price for the timber. I'll get the wagon back in time for spring planting. Everything's gonna be fine.'

Because he had said so, Johnny was utterly convinced that his problems were over. He spoke with such conviction, such reasonableness and good humour that Clem was tempted to believe him too.

More bobwhites ran out from under the trees and skittered after the others through the snow.

'Sure is a pity about them shells,' Johnny said lightly.

Clem ignored him and mounted up.

'Don't reckon I'll be more than a couple of hours,' he said.

As Johnny struggled to climb onto his horse, Clem rode forward along the path between the trees.

Instead of taking the road to Stoneheart Clem headed east across the open land towards his father's farm. The white landscape glittered in the watery light; banks of mist settled where the land fell away. Ahead of him a brace of wild turkey stepped awkwardly through the snow.

Clem hadn't been home for twelve years. Home. He could hardly call it that. He left when he was fifteen and swore he would never come back. This would be the first time Clem had faced his pa since he ran out. He smiled grimly to himself.

In his head, Clem leafed through pictures as if he had come across some old forgotten family album. He recalled fury burning in his pa's face as he stood over the body of the drifter. He remembered not understanding what had happened; he remembered nobody telling him. When he asked his ma, she looked away; when he asked his pa, he had to dodge a stinging slap across the face.

Later, after his ma died, Clem watched the farm fall into disarray. His ma would never have allowed the dogs and chickens to live in the cabin. His pa's attempts at raising livestock were half-hearted: he neglected the sheep and ill-treated the hogs. If it hadn't been for Clem nothing would have got done. His pa spent all his time in the barn with his still and eked out a living selling rotgut in town.

On his visits to sell hooch in Stoneheart, Clem's pa

drank and played poker with Sheriff Hackett, who commiserated with him because he was a good old boy whose wife had let him down.

Clem was left alone on the farm; sometimes his pa was gone for days. Clem became increasingly desperate to leave, and when the war gave him his chance he snatched it. He was grateful that the Pinkertons provided something he could believe in; more than that, he was grateful that the work kept him away.

Overhead, a red-tailed kite cut great arcs in the leaden sky. Having reached the top of the rise, Clem should have been able to see his pa's place but ice fog filled the valley gutter. Not even the rooftop was visible. A line of black chimney smoke climbed up through the mist; apart from this everything was still.

Like the other farmhouses in this part of the county, the place where Clem had grown up was a single-storey building with a porch that ran along the front. It was built close to a hillside where a spring broke through the rock and ran down to form a small lake in front of the house. A stand of curl willows overhung the water; even through the mist their cranberry-red branches were bright against the snow. To one side of the house there was a barn; behind it white oaks and lichen-covered persimmons climbed the slope.

As he entered the yard Clem called out a halloo, but there was no reply. The place should have been paradise but instead the boundary fences were broken, the gate was off its hinges and the barn door hung at an angle. In front of the house a porch post had been wrenched to one side by some animal that had been tied there. This had loosened the roof and several planks hung down unattached at one end. Blood and feathers lay scattered on the snow in front of the door to the house; the tracks of a fox circled the yard.

Human footprints crossed the yard from the cabin to the barn; hoofprints led from the barn to the track which led to the Stoneheart road. Clem called out again. No reply. He rode up to the house and dismounted. The door was ajar. A grey fox ran out, streaked across the yard and disappeared into the trees.

Inside the cabin, a chair lay on its side, blankets had been dragged off the bed; empty bottles were scattered in front of the hearth where the remains of a fire smouldered. The place was snowed with feathers as if a pillow had burst; there was blood everywhere. A half-eaten chicken carcass lay on the bed. Planted in the centre of the wooden table was an old high-back saddle. The tooling was worn smooth on the skirts, the cover had come away from the duck-bill horn and the leather stirrups had seen better days.

There was only one other place to look. Clem headed for the barn. The still was there and the whole building smelled of a new mash. His pa must have gone into Stoneheart.

Before he mounted up again Clem remembered Johnny, humiliated by having to ride bareback with his home-made bridle. He went into the house and helped himself to the saddle, heaved it up onto his

47

horse and climbed up after it. He would drop the saddle back at Johnny's cabin, then head straight into town.

He had to find some way of helping his friend settle his debts, Clem reflected. If things went on like this Johnny would starve to death. Besides that, Clem knew his pa's bullying ways. If he had teamed up with Hackett, they would steal the farm from under him. Johnny wouldn't have a chance.

It was an hour's ride from Johnny's place to Stoneheart. The mist that clung to the ground faded as the day brightened; a pale sun lifted the cold from the air. A kite wheeled high above him with the morning light glancing off its wings.

Stoneheart was two rows of wooden buildings which faced each other across an icy street. Wind had blown drifts of snow up against the walls and the smell of woodsmoke hung in the air. Everywhere, doors and windows were closed tight. Clem handed over his horse to the old-timer who swept out the livery stable.

Nothing had changed since his childhood except the scale. Time had shrunk the buildings. Doorways were lower, porches were narrower and the alleys between the stores, which had been broad enough for him and Johnny to run freely, were barely wide enough for a man to pass.

Clem recalled standing beside Johnny, their noses pressed to the store window as they ogled the jars of candies on the shelves. He used to stand and watch old Ma Passmore work the loom, which took up one half of the store, while her husband saw to the customers. On summer mornings Passmore, bald as a cue ball himself, would bring a chair out onto the porch and offer haircuts for five cents a time.

The store was the hub of town life; everyone went there. The supply wagon from St Louis would bring special deliveries; riders from other towns would leave messages; strangers passing though would make it their first port of call. It was where you bought whatever you wanted; it was where you found out whatever you needed to know.

Clem pictured twelve-year-old Sarah Lee walking down the street to the sheriff's office with her father's lunch in a wicker basket. Her smile lit the street like sunshine. He used to want her to notice him so badly, but every time he tried to say something to her his words stumbled in his mouth. He remembered waiting on the corner of the street when he knew she would pass by; when she did, she barely spared him a glance.

In all the years he'd spent away, Clem had rarely stayed in one place for more than a few weeks at a time. During the lonely times he used to think back to his home town and tried to imagine how the lives of his friends had turned out. In his mind, Johnny had become prosperous with flocks on the hills all summer; Sarah Lee was married with a team of little 'uns trailing after her apron strings.

While Clem worked for the Pinkertons he was doing right and fighting wrong. Back in Stoneheart, right and wrong hardly seem to matter; life went on anyway. Hackett bullied everyone; his pa kept the place awash with rotgut; Johnny frittered his life away at the poker table. Sarah Lee still carried her father's lunch in a wicker basket.

Clem stepped up on the porch of the saloon and pushed open the door. A pillow of warm air held the smell of tobacco and whiskey. It was a small room; someone had had the idea of arranging mirrors behind the bar to make it seem double the size. The clock was still there, the tables had been moved around, but apart from that it was as Clem remembered.

In the far corner at a table between the bar and the stove, a poker game was going on. The players studied their hands and didn't look up. Hackett sat facing the bar with his back to the stove. Next to him was Clem's pa. Johnny sat across the table from Hackett. Both Hackett and Clem's pa had piles of chips in front of them; the table in front of Johnny was empty. Zac Carter chewed a matchstick and watched the game. He was the first to notice Clem.

'Hey!'

The card players turned. Clem's pa stared at him with rheumy blue eyes. His cheeks were flushed with broken veins under a week's growth of white stubble. He carried more weight than when Clem had last seen him. He had always been a tall, strong man, now the jowls round his throat had thickened and his shoulders looked thin against his vast belly. When he recognized who stood there, his lips set in a sneer and he turned back to the game.

50

Hackett glared at Clem. He too was heavily built and strong. He was clean-shaven apart from a heavy moustache fringed with grey; his dark eyes took in everything about Clem, his height, the way he stood upright, the Colt on his hip.

Johnny's usual boyish grin had gone; his face was pinched and pale. He looked afraid. Whether this was shock because Clem had caught him at the card table or whether it was just because he was losing again, Clem couldn't tell.

'We don't want Pinkertons here,' Hackett snarled. 'We got our own law enforcement.'

'I quit,' Clem said. 'Ain't with the agency no more.'

Clem's pa turned to stare at him.

'What do you mean?'

'I quit the Pinkertons,' Clem said.

The old man hesitated while he took this in.

'Now you've come crawling back here after all this time?'

He reached in his pocket for his pouch of Bull Durham and rolled a cigarette between his thick fingers. He looked up at Clem.

'Is that it?'

'We got word the Pinks murdered a child over at Kearney,' Hackett said.

He placed his cards face down on the table. Clem hesitated.

'I was there,' he said.

The men gasped. A match flared briefly as Clem's pa lit his cigarette.

'You know Zerelda James had to have her hand

51

amputated?' Hackett went on.

'I didn't know that,' Clem said.

'That's right. Pinks didn't stick around to see what they'd done,' Hackett said.

Clem's pa exhaled a column of smoke; a cough rattled in his chest.

'Them's Missouri people,' Hackett went on. 'Zerelda was a hard-working woman. Archie was a simple-minded kid who couldn't hardly tie his own bootlaces.'

Hackett glared at him.

'Pinks threw incendiary bombs into a Missouri farmhouse in the middle of the night. They're the law-breakers.'

'I told you I quit,' Clem said.

Hackett leaned back in his chair. 'Frank and Jesse weren't even there.'

'Pinkertons betrayed Missouri people during the war.' Clem's pa coughed again. 'Still doing it now.'

'You ain't welcome here,' Hackett said. 'Better get back on your horse and ride back to wherever you've come from.'

'Ain't leaving without Johnny,' Clem said.

A sour smile crossed Hackett's face. He looked at Clem's pa.

'He thinks he can walk in here and break up our poker game,' Hackett said.

'Get out, boy.' Clem's pa shook his head in disbelief. 'Before us Missouri men throw you out.'

5

'Coming?' Clem said.

Johnny pushed his chair back from the table. Before he could get to his feet, Clem's pa slapped a meaty hand on his arm and held him still.

'We ain't finished the game,' he said.

'Don't matter,' Clem said. 'Johnny ain't playing.'

Hackett's face set in a sneer.

'He came into town to get a price for his timber,' Clem said. 'One of you must have leaned on him.'

'Leaned on him?' Clem's pa laughed. 'He begged us to let him use his timber as a stake. When we've played out this hand, an acre of it'll be mine.'

'One more hand and I'll have the other acre,' Hackett said. A narrow smile slid across his lips.

'Johnny's coming with me,' Clem said.

He leaned over, grabbed Johnny by the arm and hauled him to his feet. Clem's pa held his other arm.

'No,' Johnny protested. He tried to shake Clem off. 'You got to let me win. They're bluffing. I got a good hand this time.'

'I'm not letting you lose.'

Clem pulled Johnny away from the table.

Hackett jumped to his feet. Clem's pa yelled something. Cards and chips went flying. Across the table, Zac shouted. Johnny wrenched himself free.

'I'm gonna win this time,' Johnny yelled. 'My luck's gonna change.'

'That's right,' Hackett echoed.

The men's laughter sounded like yelping hounds.

Clem shoved Johnny back towards the door. Johnny fought back.

'Leave me be.'

Clem swung a punch which cracked Johnny's jaw. Bewilderment flashed across his face, his legs buckled and he collapsed forward into Clem's arms. Clem caught him and heaved him out into the street.

Zac pushed the other men aside and flung himself after them. With one arm holding Johnny, Clem drew his gun and levelled it at Zac's belly.

'Keep back.'

Zac glared at them from the doorway of the saloon.

'You won't be able to nursemaid him for ever,' Hackett bayed. 'He'll think he can win it all back. Never knowed him stay away from a game for more than a couple of days.'

Johnny groaned as the cold air started to revive him. Clem backed down the street, hauling Johnny with him, and kept his gun levelled at the saloon door. When he got as far as the store Clem pulled him inside.

Sarah Lee was standing at the counter talking to Ma

Passmore. A box of shotgun shells and a coil of rope stood on the counter in front of her. She shrank back when she saw the gun in Clem's hand.

Beside the door was a chair with a towel folded across the back and a tin mug containing a razor and shaving-brush. Clem swept this onto the floor and sat Johnny down. His head lolled forward and he groaned again. Clem holstered his gun.

Sarah Lee ran over and cradled Johnny's head in her hands.

'What happened?'

Clem checked the window to make sure Zac hadn't followed them.

'You did this?' Sarah Lee sounded horrified.

She knelt in front of Johnny and smoothed his forehead. His eyes flickered open for a second.

'Didn't have a choice,' Clem said.

Ma Passmore bustled out from the back room with a bottle of salts in her hand. She uncorked it and waved it under Johnny's nose. He spluttered and jolted himself upright.

'I'll fix him a cup of coffee,' she said.

Johnny tenderly brushed his palm against the side of his face. He looked up at Clem.

'Did you hit me?'

'I'm taking you home,' Clem said. 'Just one thing I've got to do first.' He looked at Sarah Lee. 'Don't let him out of your sight.'

Clem pushed open the door and stepped out into the street. Cloud banked over the town made the light grey; the air was sharp. Beyond the saloon the clang of a blacksmith's hammer rang out from the forge like a tolling bell.

This street had seemed a mile long when Clem was a kid; it was strange to discover he could pass each of the wooden buildings in a few paces. He pictured Sarah Lee again, hand in hand with her ma as she passed by.

When Clem came to the saloon door, he strode straight in. Sheriff Hackett, Clem's pa and Zac were seated at the same table. The cards were stacked, a bottle of redeye and glasses stood in front of them. Clem caught his own stern-faced reflection in one of the mirrors behind the bar. Shocked to see him, the men pushed their chairs back from the table; Zac jumped to his feet.

'Got something to tell you, Pa,' Clem announced.

His father stared at him.

'Took back the saddle.'

'What?'

The old man's eyes popped as he struggled to understand.

'You don't need it,' Clem said casually, as if an explanation was barely necessary.

'Took it?' Blood beat in the old man's face; the words caught in his throat. As his hands gripped the edge of the table the knuckles whitened. For a second it looked as though he was about to upend it: cards, glasses, everything.

'From my house?'

Clem stood still and watched fury fill his pa's face. He remembered this from when he was a kid, the way rage rose in him. Clem used to stand his ground for as long as he could and judge when it was time to get out of the way.

'I won that fair and square right here at this table,' his pa spat. 'You taken to thieving now?'

'You don't need it,' Clem repeated. 'You've cleaned him out of everything he owns.'

'The law says it was won fair and square,' Hackett said.

'What the law says and what's right ain't always the same thing.'

All three of them were shouting then. Zac yelled to be allowed to take Clem on; his pa bawled at Hackett to do something; Hackett roared about him being the law, not Clem. They kicked their chairs away and leapt to their feet; the whiskey bottle jumped off the table and spun on the floor; redeye sprayed across the room; glasses smashed; cards showered everywhere. Zac pushed between the others and ran at Clem; Clem yanked a chair out from under a table, launched it under Zac's feet, skittled his legs away and sent him crashing to the floor.

By the time Zac had picked himself up and the others had stopped shouting, Clem's gun was in his hand.

'Johnny ain't playing no more poker,' he said calmly.

'You come back here thinking you can tell us what to do?' his pa yelled. 'Telling us who can play poker and who can't? Who do you think you are?'

Zac sat down heavily on a table; he clutched his arm

57

and winced with pain.

'Nearly busted my arm.'

He grimaced; colour had drained from his face.

'If that boy don't want to play poker,' Clem's pa ranted on, 'he can say so himself. Anyhow, I mean to win that farm off him. He ain't put up the deeds yet but he will.'

'Ain't got no more collateral from what I can see,' Hackett said. 'Don't pay his debts neither. Creditors have to ride out there and take what's owed.' He laughed. 'That's the law; that's what's right. And you know it.'

'Keep away from him,' Clem said.

He backed through the door and into the street. Hackett stormed after him. As Clem stood in the cold, Hackett raged at him.

'You think we won't touch you because you'll bring your Pinkerton friends down here?'

Clem's gun was in his hand; Hackett gave no sign that he was about to draw.

'I told you,' Clem insisted. 'I left the Pinkertons.'

'You expect us to believe they wouldn't be down here if they thought you had trouble? There ain't nothing better they'd like than to take on us Southern boys.'

'What are you saying?'

Clem still expected Hackett to go for his gun.

'It was the same in the war,' Hackett jeered. 'It's the same now.'

Clem struggled to understand.

'You've lived down here too long,' he said. 'When

58

the war ended, everything changed.'

Hackett wouldn't be distracted.

'There's men round here who won't be put off by the Pinkertons or nobody,' he yelled. 'You ain't gonna get away with nothing.'

Hackett turned back into the saloon and slammed the door behind him. The cold air bit Clem's face. He holstered his gun and headed for the store.

'You told them what?'

Johnny sat in the barber's chair. The coffee mug rattled as he put it on the floor beside him.

'You shouldn't have took that saddle,' he said. 'And you shouldn't have took it to my place. They'll be down there like wolves.'

Clem stared down at him.

'This is all going to stop,' Clem said. 'Or you won't have no farm left.'

'You want to help me,' Johnny went on, 'front me a stake and I'll win it back.'

'You told me you were going to quit,' Clem said.

'Ain't got a choice.' Johnny appealed to him. 'I got to go on.'

'Listen to Clem,' Sarah Lee said.

She went and stood behind him and rested her hands lightly on his shoulders.

'He's talking sense.'

Johnny looked up at her.

'I've told you,' he said helplessly. 'I know I can win it back.'

Hoofbeats sounded in the street outside. They all

turned to the store window. Zac galloped past, head down, a scarf pulled over his face against the cold.

'Where's he headed?' Clem wondered.

'Ain't my place,' Johnny said. 'That's the opposite direction.'

'Drink up your coffee, Johnny.' Sarah Lee patted him on the shoulders. 'At least we don't have to worry about him.'

Watching Sarah Lee smile down at Johnny, Clem saw her fondness for him. She stood close behind him and rested her arms affectionately on his shoulders. For the most part, Clay County farmers were strong, self-interested men who were quick to act: thoughtfulness rarely troubled them. Johnny was different. He stood for cleverness and imagination: he wasn't cut out for farm life. Sarah Lee saw all that.

Sarah Lee had told Clem that she went to dances with her father's deputy; there couldn't be two people less suited. It had come as a shock to Clem to find her still living dutifully at home with her pa.

'You've got to listen to Clem.' Sarah Lee gently squeezed Johnny's shoulder. 'There ain't no one in this whole town can help you like he can.'

Johnny looked up at her.

'My pa may be the sheriff but he looks out for himself,' she continued. 'What's fair comes second to that.'

'He ain't so bad,' Johnny said. 'We've been playing poker together for a long time. Clem's pa too.'

'But you always lose,' Sarah Lee said.

'Not always,' Johnny snapped. 'Just recently luck

ain't been kind. A few months ago I won every hand.'

'You used to win and suddenly your luck changed?' Clem said.

Johnny grinned. 'Happens to everyone. That's why I got to roll up a stake,' he said. 'It'll change back.'

'Reckon Sarah Lee might be wrong,' Clem said. 'There might not be anything I can do for you.'

'Got the saddle back, didn't you?' Johnny said. 'They were mad but they didn't do nothing, did they?' He appealed to Clem again. 'Just let me sit in with them one more time.'

Clem looked out of the window at the street. He remembered this view from childhood. He recalled sunny afternoons, the baked-mud street and the wood-built stables opposite. Inside the store, he remembered, he'd heard the clack of the wooden shuttle as Ma Passmore worked the loom and the sound of women's laughter; he remembered the smell of coffee, cured bacon and the bunches of dry herbs that hung above the counter.

One time Clem's pa argued with Passmore as he tried to persuade him to buy the wooden case of redeye he held in his arms. Passmore wouldn't do it. Clem stood in the corner of the store and felt small. He remembered the angry bark of his pa's voice, the swish of women's skirts as they pushed past him to leave the store quickly; he remembered hearing Passmore threaten to call the sheriff. His pa had laughed then. He had barged through the shop doors, letting them swing wide, with the wooden box of redeye in his arms and headed down to the saloon.

Clem trailed after him.

Clem's pa dumped the box on the bar; the men laughed at him. From the look on his pa's red face, Clem knew that the barkeep had paid him less than he had asked for at the store.

Clem turned to Johnny.

'Riding home now to clean up those saws?'

Johnny hesitated.

'Or am I going to have to slug you again?'

Clem and Johnny headed outside to where their horses were tethered at the rail. Clem watched Johnny struggle to mount without his saddle. As they rode past the saloon Hackett pushed open the door and leaned in the doorway. Clem's pa stood behind him.

'You ain't getting away with this,' Hackett called.

Clem clicked his tongue and urged his horse forward.

'Zac's rode over to Kearney,' Hackett shouted after them. 'Frank and Jesse are gonna be mighty interested to know where you are. When they hear you were part of that raid, you're a dead man.'

Hackett's hoarse laughter echoed over the icy ground. Clem pulled his scarf over his face and did not look back.

6

Back in his cabin Johnny ran his hand over the saddle. The familiar worn leather felt good.

'Can't believe you did that,' he said.

'Fire's gone out,' Clem said. 'I'll relight it.'

He knelt in front of the grate and used his knife to shave a pile of wood flakes. He made a spark with his flint, cupped his hands round the shavings and blew on them until the spark glowed and a tiny flame caught.

Johnny sat at the table and examined the rusty saw blades.

'Have these finished tomorrow.'

The usual cheeriness had returned to his voice.

'Never intended to sell that timber, did you?' Clem said.

Clem stood up and watched as the fire gathered strength.

Johnny laughed: there was something Clem hadn't understood.

'You know I did. We talked about it.'

The fire crackled as Clem balanced a couple of split logs on the kindling. Clem stood up and shoved his hands in his pockets; he looked hard at his old friend. Was Johnny so convincing that he had convinced himself?

'Then why did you head straight for the saloon and put the timber up as a stake?'

Johnny put down the saw and stared back. 'What are you saying?'

'I had to slug you to get you out of there,' Clem said.

'I was in the middle of a game,' Johnny laughed. 'I wasn't expecting to see you.'

'You ain't answered me,' Clem insisted. 'You never intended to negotiate a price for that timber, did you?'

Johnny held the saw up to the grey light from the window and peered at the rusty teeth.

' 'Course I did. 'Course I didn't.' Avoiding Clem's eye, Johnny continued to examine the blade. 'What difference does it make? Why are you asking me, anyway?'

Clem banged his fist on the table; the two-hander jumped across the wood. He glared at his old friend.

'Gonna slug me again?' Johnny jeered. 'That make you feel better?'

Clem said nothing.

'What is it you want to hear?' Johnny threw the saw down. 'I intended to get a price for the timber; I intended to head straight for the saloon.'

'What's the matter with you?' Clem said. 'You gonna sit there and let them take this place off you?'

'I win sometimes,' Johnny said. 'When I do, I wipe the grins off their greedy faces. You don't know how good that feels.'

Clem stared at him.

'I'm better than them. I remember the hands. I calculate the odds. I'm fast.' Johnny pushed the saw aside. His words tumbled out before Clem could interrupt. 'I ain't much of a farmer; I ain't the sheriff and I ain't got a whiskey still. But I can do that.'

'You lose,' Clem reminded him. 'You've been losing for a long time.'

Johnny stared out of the window. Melting snow dripped from the edge of the roof.

'Lady Luck ran out on me,' he said. 'She'll be back.'

'That's your plan?' Clem said. 'To wait for a lucky streak?'

Johnny grinned; he didn't hear the irony in Clem's words; he relaxed. *Roll on that lucky streak*, he thought. *Can't be much longer. Law of averages.*

'Every time I walk into that saloon and see Hackett there in his same old seat with his back to the stove, I think: today's the day.'

Warmth filled the room now; the fire crackled encouragingly. Johnny leaned back in his chair.

'A year ago I asked Sarah Lee to marry me.'

Johnny's voice was low. He had decided to confide in Clem but was not sure that he should.

'Sarah Lee?'

'She didn't say yes; she didn't say no,' Johnny went on.

Clem waited for him to spill the rest of the story.

65

'Her pa wouldn't agree,' Johnny said. 'Said I wasn't good enough.'

Johnny levered himself out of his seat and threw another log on the fire. Sparks burst up the chimney.

'Said he didn't want me to have nothing to do with her. Said he wouldn't ever change his mind.'

'What are you gonna do about it?'

'What can I do?'

Orange flames licked round the new log as the edges of the bark caught and flared. Beads of sap hissed where the wood had been sawn.

Clem held up his hand for Johnny to be quiet. He pushed back his chair and crossed to the window.

'Thought I heard something.'

They both stared out into the yard. Patches of mud showed through the snow; water dripped from the trees.

Clem unholstered his Colt. He nodded towards the shotgun, which stood beside the door where he had left it.

'Did you pick up a box of shells at the store?'

'Intended to,' Johnny said. His voice sounded hollow. 'Never made it.'

Clem studied the tree line. Nothing had changed except that the bobwhites' tracks had softened as the snow thawed.

'Sure I heard something,' Clem said. 'The path through the woods, that's the only way up to the Stoneheart road?'

'Unless you cut across country.'

'Swear I heard a rider,' Clem breathed.

'Couldn't have done,' Johnny said. 'If someone had been in the trees they'd be here by now.'

Clem stood to one side of the window as if he expected a shot. Johnny peered over his shoulder.

'How long does it take to get to Kearney if you ride hard?' Clem asked.

'You think it's Frank and Jesse?' Johnny's words dried his throat.

'How long?'

'Half a day if you know the route,' Johnny said. 'Couldn't be them. Zac hasn't had time.'

'Could have been on their way,' Clem said. 'Someone could have told them where I was.'

They stood still. The only thing they could hear was the fizz of the wet log in the fire. Clem pulled back the hammer on his Colt.

'I'm going out to take a look.'

'Could be waiting for you to do that like the Pinks at Kearney,' Johnny said.

Clem hesitated for a second.

'I'm going anyway.'

'I'm coming,' Johnny said. 'I'll bring the shotgun. They don't know it ain't loaded.'

Clem grabbed his arm. They froze. Then they both heard it. A horse whinnied somewhere behind the tree line.

'When I open the door you go left, I go right,' Clem said.

Johnny nodded and grabbed the shotgun. Clem's hand was on the door handle. He glanced at Johnny.

'Don't stop till you reach the trees.'

Clem threw open the door. They kept low and ran.

Slush slipped under Clem's boots; cold air scratched his face; at any second he expected the whine of a pistol shot. Ice cracked and mud splashed up as he leapt the stream. He shouldered into the trees; branches whipped at him. As he threw himself against the trunk of an oak, breath exploded in his chest. He stood still and strained to catch a sound above the banging of his heart against his ribs. He could hear Johnny stumbling through the brush on the other side of the yard and the patter of thawing snow on the icy ground. Nothing more.

Clem peered round the trunk of the oak again, ready to jerk back at the sound of a shot. The woods were empty. Pale sunlight filtered through the branches; thawing snow pattered on the icy ground.

With his Colt ready, Clem held up an arm to shield his face from low branches and pressed further into the woods. No sign of anyone. No sound. He headed in the direction of the track which led to the Stoneheart road. Briars snatched at his clothes; the snowy brushwood was waist high in places. Melting snow fell on his shoulders; water dripped off the brim of his hat.

Then Clem saw her. A bay mare stood on the track; steam rose off her back and her breath was a cloud in front of her face. No rider. Clem scanned the trees. The mare ducked her head: for a moment, Clem thought she was grazing. Two steps closer and he caught sight of the body face down on the ground.

The horse nudged the rider as if he had fallen

asleep in the snow and she wanted to wake him. She raised her head and took a pace back to let Clem get close. He shoved his gun into its holster and gently pulled at the shoulder of the fallen man. It was Zac.

Clem felt for a pulse. He leaned over Zac's face; his breathing was soft and shallow. Clem eased him over onto his back. His jacket and shirt were dark; the snow was red where he lay. He had been shot in the chest.

Johnny crashed through the brush.

'Ain't no one here,' he said. 'I've looked around.'

He gasped when he saw Zac's body.

'Lost a lot of blood,' Clem said.

Between them they lifted him as gently as they could and carried him along the path to the cabin. The mare trailed after them.

Inside, with Zac stretched out on the bed, Johnny built up the fire while Clem peeled back his clothes to look at the wound. Two slugs, close together, just below and to the left of the heart.

Zac's skin was damp with sweat. His eyes remained closed. Each breath rattled his chest. Clem cut him out of his wet shirt, eased off his boots and covered him with a blanket. He supported his head and held a cup of melted snow to his lips. Zac managed a few sips before the water ran down his chin and Clem let him lie back.

'Reckon Jesse James did this?' Johnny asked.

He spoke softly so as not to wake the wounded man. If Jesse James had done this, that would mean he was close. Clem heard fear echo in Johnny's voice. He didn't answer.

'What are we gonna do?' Johnny persisted.

'Take his gun,' Clem said. 'If Jesse James comes you'll need it.'

Johnny buckled on Zac's Colt.

'Got to get those slugs out,' Clem said. 'If we leave 'em he'll die for sure.'

Zac's breathing was light. Already a dark stain showed on the blanket; he still had not opened his eyes.

The skillet was slow to boil; Clem cleaned the blade of his hunting knife. Even though Zac's forehead was hot to the touch and his skin glistened with sweat, he shivered beneath the blanket.

Johnny had moved a chair to one side of the window. With Zac's Colt ready on his knees, he stared out.

'You'll have to help me,' Clem said. 'I'll need you to hold him.'

Johnny continued to stare out of the window.

'Reckon he'd do the same for me?'

'If you were lying there, I'd be asking him to pin you down,' Clem said.

Bubbles started to appear round the edge of the skillet. Clem dropped in his hunting knife, then went to kneel by the bedside.

'Zac, can you hear me?'

Clem shook him lightly.

Zac's eyelids were blue and the veins showed through the skin; his eye sockets were dark as though someone had daubed them in charcoal; the skin on

70

his face clung to his skull. For a second his eyes moved even though the lids remained closed. The note of his breathing changed as if a word was trying to pass through his lips.

'Who shot you, Zac?' Clem persisted.

Zac lay still, his breathing caught in his chest. He didn't open his eyes.

The water bubbled in the skillet. Clem slipped Zac's belt from round his waist, folded it twice and set it down by the bed. He fished his hunting knife out of the boiling water.

'You're gonna have to help me,' Clem said. 'Make him bite on the belt, then hold his shoulders down.'

Johnny took a last look out of the window. Clem studied the neat bullet holes and noted the way the slugs had smashed through the ribs.

As Johnny passed Clem the skillet from the grate they both heard it. Someone else was in the woods. There was no attempt to disguise it; the hoofbeats were loud and fast. Johnny grabbed the Colt and crossed the cabin to the window. Clem followed.

Neither of them spoke. There was no time to hide, no time to do anything. The rider kept coming. They could hear branches breaking; hoofbeats stamped on the ground.

'Hey.' Zac's voice was a scratch in his throat.

Clem turned. Zac lay with his head on its side, his eyes open.

'I left a message for Frank and Jesse so they'd know where to find you.'

He laughed. The laugh exploded into a cough

which bucked his chest, lifted him half off the bed and threw him down. Blood filled his mouth and spattered the blanket when he breathed. He lay still and stared at them.

Zac tried to speak again but Clem turned back to the window. Johnny thumbed back the hammer of his Colt. The rider crashed through the brush into the yard.

7

'Anyone there?'

Sarah Lee jumped down from her appaloosa and burst through the saloon door.

'Pa's just had word from the sheriff at Kearney.' Out of breath, her words fell over each other. 'Jesse James found out there was an undercover Pinkerton working on the neighbour's farm, pretending to be a farm hand.' She stared at Clem. 'Rode out there and shot him stone dead.'

Clem pulled up a chair and sat down.

'Pa says he would have shot the farmer too if he hadn't known him all his life.'

Johnny turned to Clem.

'Know anything about this?'

'Jesse said this Pinkerton was the one who was responsible for the raid when Archie got killed,' Sarah Lee went on.

'There was an undercover up there,' Clem said. 'He'd been watching the James place for weeks. Gave us the word that Frank and Jesse were there.'

Clem stared out of the window. Thawing snow fell from the branches of the trees like rain.

Zac tried to laugh. A tight sound strangled his throat. Sarah Lee turned and saw him for the first time. There was a wide patch of blood on the blanket.

'Zac, what happened?'

She looked into his face, stepped over quickly and lifted the blanket. The two dark holes oozed blood. Then she saw the skillet of steaming water and Clem's hunting knife with the handle wrapped in cotton on the chair by the bed.

'What's going on? Who did this?'

She had walked in on something and struggled to understand what it was.

'We found him in the woods,' Johnny said. 'Brought him in.'

'You were riding to Kearney?' Sarah Lee asked.

Zac's face shone with sweat; his eyelids fluttered; he groaned as if he was holding up some great weight. Sarah Lee focused on the knife by the bed.

'What were you going to do with that?'

'Got to get the slugs out,' Clem said.

'With a hunting knife?' Sarah Lee's anger flared. 'Do you want to kill him? This ain't the frontier. There's a doctor in Stoneheart now.' Sarah Lee glared at Johnny. 'Why didn't you fetch him?'

'You know no one in town will talk to me. Clem said he could. . . .' Johnny hesitated.

'Fetch him.' Sarah Lee's voice was cold. 'Now.'

'I guess I'll. . . .'

Johnny glanced at Clem, slipped his arm under the

saddle which sat in the centre of the table and headed outside.

'I could go,' Clem said.

'You stay here.' She handed him the knife. 'Put that thing away. I don't know why he didn't tell you about the doctor.'

'Does he owe him money?' Clem said.

Sarah Lee brushed the question aside.

'You know who did this?'

Johnny shook his head.

'Better find out or my pa is likely to blame you. Seen how close together those slugs are? Whoever put them there was a good shot. Everyone knows Johnny can hardly hit a barn door.'

Sarah Lee lifted the skillet off the chair and sat next to the bed. She smoothed Zac's forehead and brushed his cheek with the back of her hand. His eyes moved beneath the lids.

'Can you hear me?'

His lips moved soundlessly; his eyes stayed closed.

'Who did this, Zac?'

His lips moved again but there were no words.

Clem picked up Zac's shirt, went outside and packed one of the sleeves with snow. When he came back inside Zac's eyes were open; he stared up into Sarah Lee's face. Sarah Lee held the ice first against one temple then the other. Then she held it over his mouth; water droplets fell onto his lips.

'Who did this, Zac?'

'Met a guy on the road who said he knew where Jesse was.'

Zac's voice was paper dry.

'Told him there was a Pinkerton holed up outside Stoneheart.'

'He shot you for that?'

Sarah Lee held the ice against Zac's cheek. Breath rattled in his throat and flecks of blood appeared on his lips.

'Saw my tin star.'

His glazed eyes wandered over to where Clem stood by the window. Clem pondered what Zac had said.

'That ain't it,' Clem said slowly. 'You asked for money. How much did you want for telling him where I was?'

Zac didn't answer; when he looked at Clem his eyes were empty.

'First you ride up to Kearney wearing a deputy's star,' Clem said. 'Then you demand a price for information wanted by Frank and Jesse James. Don't you know how close people are up there?'

Zac closed his eyes. Sarah Lee touched his temples with the ice; his breathing steadied.

'Did you get the name of the guy who shot you?' Clem insisted.

Zac didn't answer.

While they waited for Johnny and the doctor Sarah Lee made Clem move some of the logs out of the grate onto the stone hearth.

'He's burning up. No sense in making him hotter.'

Zac didn't say anything else, nor did he open his eyes. By the time Dr Hanson rode in with Sheriff Hackett he was dead.

'Where's Johnny?' Clem said.

'Following on,' Hackett said curtly. 'Said something about needing shotgun shells.'

Hackett stood with his back to the door, his hand resting on the handle of his Colt. He ignored Clem and glared at his daughter. Sarah Lee backed into a corner of the room and kept her eyes on the doctor.

Hanson was a tall man in a black jacket and a gravy-stained shirt. He lifted the blanket and gave the body an impatient glance. He didn't bother to bend down to inspect the wounds.

'Two shots to the chest like that.' He shrugged. 'Surprised he made it this far.'

'Did he say anything?' Hackett said.

'Said he met someone on the road and told him there was a Pinkerton in these parts,' Clem said. 'When the fella saw his deputy's badge, he shot him.'

'If Stoneheart is about to get a visit from the great Jesse James, we best find out what the reward stands at,' Hackett said. 'You going to get word to your Pinkerton buddies so they can set up another ambush?'

'Keep telling you,' Clem said, 'I quit.'

'Won't make no difference to Jesse when he catches you.' Hackett smirked.

'Pa,' Sarah Lee said. Her face was bright with anger. 'What are you saying?'

Hackett rounded on her. 'I told you before not to come out here. Zac was a good man. Good enough for you. Instead, what did you do? Dressed in farmer's clothes and hung around with a broke gambler who

77

reads books.' The contempt in his voice made Sarah Lee look away. 'The James boys are coming,' Hackett went on. 'They'll get rid of this Pinkerton whether he's quit or not.'

As if she hadn't heard, Sarah Lee turned towards the grate and busied herself building up the fire.

'You can collect the certificate from my office,' Hanson broke in. 'Want me to send Passmore out here with a cart?'

Hackett moved to let Hanson open the door and followed him outside. The men climbed onto their horses. Cushions of grey cloud filled the sky; the branches of the hickories were black and wet; the air was still sharp.

'James brothers come calling, I'll tell 'em where to find you,' Hackett jeered.

Clem pushed the door shut before the sheriff had finished speaking.

'Johnny should be back,' Clem said.

Sarah Lee stood up.

'What do you mean?'

From the window, Clem watched Hackett disappear into the woods.

'We'll give 'em time to get ahead, then we'll ride into town,' said Sarah Lee.

She set about tidying Johnny's few possessions. She straightened the small pile of charred books by the bed, folded the top of the bean sack closed and picked up an onion that had fallen on the floor.

'Fond of him, ain't you?' Clem said.

'Just sick of seeing him pushed around.' Sarah Lee

stared into the skillet and watched the surface of the water move.

'He should have left this place a long time ago,' she went on. 'Just packed up and left it all behind.'

'Could have sold the farm,' Clem said.

'Who to?' Sarah Lee looked at him. 'Think your pa would have given him a fair price?'

'Could have put it with an agent.'

'They would have found some way of scaring off a buyer.' Then she added, 'As soon as he takes his seat at a poker game, they know it's just a question of time. They'll clean him out of everything eventually.'

They waited an hour. Clem pulled the blanket over Zac's face and moved two chairs up to the grate.

'Should feel sad, shouldn't I?' Sarah Lee said. 'I went to dances with him.'

She stared into the flames.

Later, as they mounted up, Sarah Lee said, 'I thought of running away with Johnny once, packing up his books and a few blankets and heading for Kansas.'

'Why didn't you?'

'Who would have kept house for Pa?' Sarah Lee turned her horse into the woods. 'Anyway, we weren't even sweethearts.'

Melted snow had soaked the dirt; dark mud clung to the hoofs of the horses.

'So I started rearing ponies,' she said. 'Johnny went back to poker.'

She hesitated.

'He's always played, right from when he was a kid.

Now it was like playing was his life. He won too, beat everyone. Didn't keep quiet about it neither. You know what he's like; if he's got an idea in his head he wants to share it with the world.'

Sarah Lee's voice softened; she stared straight ahead. Clem pulled his horse closer. 'Then they all started to gang up on him, my pa, your pa, practically everyone who'd ever played cards in the saloon.'

'Didn't he have enough winnings to pull out by then?'

Sarah Lee laughed. 'Should have. Half the time, when someone owed him money, he'd forget to collect or the guy would come up with some hard-luck story and Johnny would just smile and tell him to forget about it.'

'Didn't collect what he was owed?' Clem said. 'What kind of gambler does that?'

'With Johnny it's the playing,' Sarah Lee said. 'It ain't the winning; it ain't even the money.'

They came out of the woodland. Dull clouds clogged the sky; the horses splashed along the muddy track; in the hillsides, dirt scars showed where the snow had melted.

'He can't pass the saloon door without looking in to see if someone will let him sit in on a game. He keeps asking but only my pa and your pa will play with him now. No one else has time for him.'

'He owes them too,' Clem said. 'He told me.'

'They want his farm,' Sarah Lee said. 'Ain't gonna stop till they get it.'

When they reached the crest of the hill they joined

the Stoneheart road. A line of black mud stretched ahead of them. An hour's ride away, smoke from the town chimneys rose over the far hill.

'What about you?' Sarah Lee said. 'You got away.'

'Ran away,' Clem said. 'Never thought I'd be back here. Thought I'd be working for the agency for ever.'

'Must have been bad over at Kearney.'

Clem stared at the horizon.

'Never knew Frank and Jesse had a ten-year-old brother till they briefed us.'

'Stepbrother,' Sarah Lee said. 'Their ma's been married three times. Their pa took off for California when they were kids to preach the word; the typhus got him out there. Second husband was real cruel to Frank and Jesse so Zerelda left him; then he died. Third husband, Dr Samuels, is Archie's pa. There's sisters too.'

Up ahead, a rider approached. He walked his horse towards them but kept a hundred yards wide of the track. Neither Clem nor Sarah Lee could say whether the rider had seen them. His hat was pulled down against the weather and he was hunched low on his horse. When he got closer they saw that the rider had wrapped his arms around himself to try to keep warm. He wasn't wearing a jacket.

Clem reined in his horse and stood still.

'Johnny,' Clem hallooed him.

He must have heard but he didn't turn. He kept on riding straight ahead parallel with the road.

'Johnny,' Clem called again.

Again Johnny ignored him. As he passed them,

even from this distance they could see that he rode bareback.

Sarah Lee watched as Clem turned his horse. He galloped hard in case Johnny had any thoughts of taking flight. Clem rode straight at him, hauled on his reins when he got close and leapt out of his saddle.

Johnny turned towards him as if he was in a dream, as if he hadn't heard the thunderous hoofbeats, as if he didn't recognize his friend who pulled him off his horse and threw him onto the frozen ground. He stared up at Clem as if the words he was shouting at him were in some language he didn't understand. When Clem reached down, grabbed his shirt and hauled him upright Johnny offered no resistance; when Clem flung back his fist ready to break his jaw, he did not move away.

Sarah Lee was there then. She flung herself on Clem's arm to stop the punch. They were both shouting. Clem yelled; Sarah Lee screamed at Clem to stop. As Clem tried to take the swing, the weight of Sarah Lee clinging to his arm unbalanced them both and they toppled backwards.

Johnny stared at them as if he didn't understand what they were doing there.

Clem struggled to his feet.

'Ain't you ever gonna quit?'

'Clem,' Sarah Lee warned. 'Don't.'

Johnny's expression was innocent surprise, as though Sarah Lee and Clem had walked into his house without knocking. His arms clung to himself; his face was grey with cold.

'I was winning,' he said. 'I couldn't fail. I remembered all the hands. I thought Lady Luck had sat down beside me.'

He seemed to be talking to himself, not to them.

'Then every time I was about to clean up, they folded. It was real quick.'

'What are you saying?' Clem said.

Johnny stared from one to the other of them. His voice was no more than a whisper.

'I lost it all.'

8

Hackett leaned in the doorway of the sheriff's office as Clem and the others rode into town. He narrowed his eyes and took the stogie from between his lips.

'You still here?' he called.

Clem reined in his horse.

'I heard the James brothers is killing Pinks for sport after what they did,' Hackett continued. 'Ain't gonna be long before they're right here asking where you are. I'm likely to be the one who is gonna tell 'em.' Hackett's laugh rumbled in his chest. 'That's if your pa don't tell 'em first.'

Clem wheeled his horse over to the saloon, dismounted and tied it to the rail. Johnny and Sarah Lee followed. Hackett levered himself off the doorpost and stared after them.

The snow had disappeared from the Stoneheart street and left a river of cloying mud. As soon as Clem and the others climbed down from their stirrups, mud stuck to their boots like tar.

Inside the saloon the air was warm. The place was

empty apart from the barkeep, who was polishing one of the mirrors behind the bar, and Clem's pa, who sat with his back to the door. On the floor beside him was Johnny's saddle; slung over the back of a chair was his jacket.

Clem strode across the room, grabbed the jacket and threw it to Johnny. His pa looked up at him. His eyes were yellow and broken veins were laced across his face.

'Been expecting you,' he said. 'Sheriff said you'd run out when you heard Frank and Jesse were comin' but I knew different. He'll go in his own time, I said. My boy's brave.'

A smile slid across Clem's pa's mouth; his eyes were still fixed on him. The bottle of redeye on the table in front of him was half empty.

'Treacherous,' he went on. 'But brave.'

'What are you talking about?' Clem said.

'You know what I'm talking about.' The old man's rheumy eyes fixed on him. 'You ran off and joined the Pinkertons. You betrayed us in the war and it ain't no different now.'

'You're drunk,' Clem said.

'Take the jacket.' Guttural laughter broke in his pa's chest. 'Take back the saddle. He'll need it. I've given him till midnight to get out.'

'What are you saying?' Clem said.

'We won his farm.' Clem's pa stared at him. 'Me and the sheriff won it fair and square at this table.'

Clem turned to Johnny. His face registered nothing.

85

'He don't know when to stop.' Clem's pa relished twisting the knife. 'He'll tell you about numbers, odds and the chances of this and that. But the truth is it's all luck and in this life you've got to make your own.'

A laugh erupted in his chest.

Hackett slammed the saloon door shut and marched over to the table; a cloud of cigar smoke followed him into the room.

'I never agreed to him taking that saddle – or the jacket for that matter,' Hackett snapped. 'Half of them winnings is mine.'

Clem's pa shrugged.

'We got half the farm. We can put a tenant in there. What do I care about a jacket?'

'It's a principle, ain't it?' Hackett said. 'You sit down to play poker, you either win or lose.'

'Pa,' Sarah Lee broke in. 'You could let him have his jacket.'

'I told you not to have anything to do with him but you ignored me.' Hackett's temper flared. 'You've wasted years trailing round after him. Now look at you.'

Sarah Lee gasped.

'I warned you, didn't I?' Hackett went on. 'You knew about his card-playing; you knew he lost every time. Who's gonna want you now?'

'How could you?' Sarah Lee burst out. Tears stood in her eyes. 'I ain't trailed round after him, I've trailed round after you.'

She stared at him. Her words were precise and clear, as though she had known what she wanted to say for a long time.

'I cooked for you, cleaned for you and kept house every day since Ma died. I listened to you railing on about loyalty and cussing the Yankees and predicting the sky was going to fall in because the South lost the war. . . .'

Hackett rounded on her.

'You're my daughter,' he thundered. 'I brought you up right. But you hung around with this no-good loser.'

'I went to dances with Zac and all the other good old boys you found for me, didn't I? I listened to them talk about how they bet they could wrestle a steer to the ground, or how they could drink a gallon of whiskey and still stand upright, or how they could hobble a pony so tight he'd break his leg if he fell.'

Sarah Lee sank down into a chair. She looked away from them all and her voice drifted.

'I listened to all of that,' she said quietly. 'Week in, week out for years.'

'You wasted your life.' Hackett's face shone with anger; his words rained on her like blows. 'You know he's worthless. Complain all you want.'

Johnny stood by the door, pale-faced and with his jacket half on. As he struggled to shove his arm into the sleeve he stared at the floor. All the strength had been leached out of him.

Silence settled on the room for a moment. The collar of Sarah Lee's saddle jacket remained turned up against the cold even though the saloon was warm. She had heard them before, but her father's words still bruised her to the bone.

Outside a horse kicked up a shower of mud as a rider passed. At the sound of the hoofbeats, the men turned towards the window. Sarah Lee didn't seem to hear anything.

'I got my appaloosas,' Sarah Lee said quietly. 'Raised two of 'em and I brung 'em on right. There's no one in this room except me can say they've done that.'

Hackett and Clem's pa knew that what Sarah Lee said was true. They were surprised that her kind way of training the horses produced results more quickly than the beatings and hobbles horse-breakers usually used. They had seen with their own eyes how loyal the ponies were to her, how they instantly responded to the gentlest of her commands and how affectionately they nuzzled against her. They respected her for this even though they begrudged showing it.

The redeye bottle clinked against the glass as Clem's pa poured himself another drink. Sarah Lee buried her hands in her jacket pockets and avoided looking at any of them.

'Your appaloosas won't save your friend who gambles his farm away.' Hackett glared at her. 'They won't save anyone when Jesse James gets here.'

'Midnight.' Clem's pa leered at Johnny. 'That's how long you got.'

Johnny's face was the colour of ash.

'You got time to clear out whatever you're taking with you. We'll be over there to take possession before sunup.'

Clem's pa slugged back his glass of redeye; laughter wheezed in his chest.

'At least we left you your horse. Otherwise you'd be walking out of here.'

'What will you do with the farm?' Johnny spoke for the first time.

Hackett and Clem's pa both turned to look at him. His face was thin; he looked ill.

'What do you want to know for?' Hackett blustered. 'You've lived there all your life. You've never been interested in the place. All you wanted was to sit at this table right here.'

Hackett felt in his vest pocket for matches and relit his stogie.

'I thought if you were going to look for a tenant, maybe I could rent it off you. I'd work hard. I know I could make a profit.'

Clem's pa wheezed a laugh.

'Hear that, Sheriff? Says he wants to work for us.'

'Midnight.' Hackett rested his hand on the pistol in his belt. 'And the farm's ours.'

The saloon door burst open. Pa Passmore stood there in his long apron, which reached from his waist to the ground. He slammed the door shut and leaned back against it to catch his breath.

'Message for the sherrif,' Passmore gasped. 'Rider from Kearney wants to know if there's any reply.'

He held out a brown envelope addressed with the words: *Sheriff, Stoneheart.*

Hackett tore open the envelope and let it fall to the floor while his eyes scanned the paper it contained.

When Hackett looked up a grin twisted his mouth.

'Official confirmation,' he said. 'Jesse James is headed this way.'

He cleared his throat and read aloud: ' "From Sheriff's Office, Kearney, Missouri, to Sheriff's Office, Stoneheart. Be advised we have today received intelligence from a representative of the Pinkerton Detective Agency, who has been trailing the fugitives Frank and Jesse James. The information states that the pair have split up. Frank James is headed north in the direction of Kansas while Jesse is riding south.

"We understand that following the unsuccessful arrest attempt at the James farm on January 26 last, the James brothers have determined to track down and murder the Pinkerton agents involved in that raid. If you are in contact with any agents in your area, please make them aware of this situation immediately." '

Hackett lowered the paper and looked at Clem.

' 'Course, when Jesse comes through here. I'll tell him not to bother you because you ain't a Pink no more. After you helped them murder his little brother, you quit. Ain't that right?'

Clem stared at him.

'Listen.' Hackett laughed. 'There's more. ' "If our intelligence is accurate, Jesse James should arrive in Stoneheart at around midnight tonight." '

Clem's pa drained his glass.

'They're gonna call me the man whose son was shot by Jesse James.'

He poured himself another drink to celebrate.

'Sure gonna be busy round here at midnight,' Clem's pa went on. 'Nobody won't be getting much shut-eye tonight.'

'You think Jesse James is gonna ride in here and be on your side?' Clem stared at Hackett. 'Ever knowed him make friends with a sheriff?'

'I'm gonna tell him where you are,' Hackett snarled. 'If you've run out by then, I'll tell him which direction you're headed.'

'You think that will stop Jesse James from shooting you stone dead?'

Hackett relit his stogie and puffed on it to show Clem he could say whatever he liked.

'Jesse James wants to put a slug in every lawman in Clay County, even rotten ones like you.'

Blue smoke wreathed around Hackett. He sat back and let Clem talk.

'I won't be wearing my sheriff's star come midnight, that's for sure,' Hackett said. 'Just as a precaution.' He grinned again. 'But say what you like, it ain't me he's after, it's you.'

Clem's pa grunted to himself. His bottle clinked against the edge of the glass.

'The other thing is: he may not come,' Clem said. 'You got no idea how many times Pinkerton intelligence is wrong. Somebody hears a rumour; somebody makes a guess; somebody else passes it on. Suddenly somebody calls it intelligence. That's what happened over at Kearney.'

'Jesse James is comin',' Hackett said. 'He's a Missouri man. You Pinkertons hurt his family. He ain't

91

never going to forget that.'

Passmore spoke up.

'Is there a reply? I got this fella drinking coffee at the store.'

Hackett stretched his legs out in front of him and took a last pull on his stogie.

'Just say that when Jesse James comes we'll be ready.'

He dropped the cigar butt on the floor and ground it under his heel.

Passmore stepped out into the muddy street.

Hackett looked up at Clem. 'I'm surprised you ain't left yet.' He pulled a fob watch out of his vest pocket.

'Six hours till midnight. That ain't much of a start when you're running from a man like Jesse James.'

He leaned forward as if he was sharing a confidence. 'Could be your last six hours on this earth.'

'I ain't running from no one,' Clem said.

Sarah Lee turned to him.

'You're staying here?'

'Looks like I'll have to face him some time,' Clem said. 'Might as well be tonight.'

'Don't reckon that's a good idea.' Johnny hadn't spoken for a while. 'There ain't nothing for you to do here now. What's the point in staying, anyway?'

'To start with, we got to get your things packed up back at the farm,' Clem said. 'Looks like you're going to be on the trail for a while.'

Johnny stared at him. His face was pinched; his jacket hung half-off his shoulders. Clem took hold of the lapels and shook him into it.

92

Clem's pa turned his back on them and reached out to pour himself another slug of redeye. Looking into the mirror behind the bar, Clem judged where the bottle was, leaned over the old man's shoulder and snatched it away.

'Hey,' Clem's pa spluttered. 'What's going on?'

'You've had enough,' Clem said curtly.

Clem's pa tried to push himself out of his seat. Clem pressed down on his shoulder, kept him there and held the bottle out of his reach. The effort meant the old man's words were lost in an angry explosion of coughing.

Sarah Lee faced Hackett. 'I'm going with them.'

'What do I care?' Hackett sneered. 'This will be the last time.'

Clem seized the saddle which sat on the floor by his pa's chair. The old man was doubled over. His breath tore at his lungs; his chest jolted and used up all the strength it would have taken to speak.

Outside, daylight fled from the sky; shadows gathered between the buildings and wind got up. The clouds moved overhead but there was no moon. Clem pulled his jacket tight to his throat. He and Sarah Lee mounted up and waited while Johnny adjusted the girth. They watched him wrestle with the task he had carried out almost every day of his life since he was a boy. He was weak: the events of the day had chastened him.

The saloon door opened. Hackett and Clem's pa stood and watched them.

'Midnight,' Hackett barked. 'We'll be there to take

93

possession. If Jesse James shows, we'll be sure to bring him with us.'

Clem upended the bottle of redeye and let the contents spill into the mud. He tossed the bottle aside and mounted up. Without a glance at the men in the doorway he wheeled his horse out into the street.

9

'Do you think he's really coming?'

Sarah Lee stood at the table in Johnny's cabin and rubbed her hands through a bowlful of sugar, flour and fat. She was making biscuits for Johnny to take with him. Clem knelt in front of the grate and rekindled the fire.

'Jesse James?' Clem said. 'Most likely on his way right now.'

Johnny drew a chair up to the hearth and waited for the warmth. He watched them work without seeming to fully understand what they were doing.

'If he killed the undercover on the next-door farm,' Clem went on, 'this will be his next stop.'

'You could be halfway to Kansas,' Sarah Lee said. 'You're sure you want to wait for him here?'

She stared down at her hands working the flour.

'If Jesse James is on your trail, you got nowhere to go,' Clem said. 'He won't give up.'

Sarah Lee splashed a cup of water into the flour.

'What about the other Pinkertons? They want to

catch him. They'd help you.'

'Ain't seen them since Kearney,' Clem said. 'How could I get word to them tonight?'

Flames licked round the logs in the grate; Johnny pulled his chair closer and stared into the fire.

Sarah Lee cut out rounds of dough, found a tin tray and balanced them over the flames. She turned to Johnny.

'Watch 'em so they don't catch. I'll turn 'em in a minute.'

He didn't look up.

'You ain't packed anything,' Sarah Lee said gently.

She pulled a watch out of her pocket, the kind the previous generation of women pinned to their dresses.

'Four hours, Johnny. Ain't you at least going to put a bedroll together?'

Johnny's attention was immersed in the flames; he didn't hear her. Sarah Lee caught Clem's eye.

'Leave him,' Clem said.

A sudden, sharp burning smell made Sarah Lee pick up a cloth and dash for the tray of biscuits. She moved it onto the stone hearth and flipped each one with a knife. Johnny stared into the fire; he gave no sign that he had noticed.

For a while they settled into uneasy silence, each lost in their own thoughts. Johnny stared at the dancing flames; Clem drew his Colt and snapped open the chamber; Sarah Lee smoothed out the dough for a second batch. But in spite of the warmth of the fire and the homely smell of baking, each of them was aware of the minutes ticking away.

Suddenly Johnny looked up. He pushed his chair back from the fire and got to his feet.

'Sarah Lee,' he said.

He laced his fingers anxiously in front of him. Sarah Lee brushed the flour off her hands.

'I let you down,' he went on. 'You were good to me for a long time. I let it all slip away.'

Sarah Lee stared down at the dough.

'Once I thought you might be my sweetheart. You remember how you used to come out here and I'd read stories to you?'

He twisted his fingers together until the joints cracked.

'You remember that, don't you?'

Sarah Lee saw weariness in his face. She saw how the realization that he had finally lost everything exhausted him.

'I loved your stories.' She smiled sadly. 'But you didn't fight for me.'

Johnny let his arms fall to his sides.

'Poker games,' he said. 'Crazy ideas of winning. It all swept me away until I couldn't think of nothing else.'

'I tried to tell you,' Sarah Lee said. 'You wouldn't listen.'

'Couldn't,' Johnny said. 'Couldn't hear nothing except the voice in my head which said everything would be all right if I was at a poker table.' He pulled his knuckles until they cracked. 'I didn't care about nothing else. Didn't care about the farm. Remember how I used to love to take a book and a fishing pole down to the river? Didn't even want to do that no more.'

Johnny raised his hands as if he was passing something to her.

'Just thought, if I could keep playing. . . .'

'How can you win if you can't stop playing?' Sarah Lee said. 'That's what I was trying to tell you.'

'I know that now.'

Johnny's hands fell to his sides again.

'I won at first,' he went on. 'Made me feel like a king. Then I couldn't stop. When they changed everything around in the saloon, I never won after that. Now I've lost it all.'

'Where will you go?'

'Guess I'll take the trail up to Kansas.' He stared at the floor. 'Plenty of farms on the way. Some of them must be wanting someone to work for a dollar a day. If I go someplace where there ain't a saloon, I might be able to roll up a stake by summer.'

He managed a smile.

'Maybe you'll be out with your ponies one August day, you'll look up and there I'll be.'

'I'd like that,' Sarah Lee said.

She crossed over to him, held him and kissed him lightly on the cheek. Then she laughed at the flour which was on his shoulders and down the front of his jacket and made a show of brushing it off.

Outside, the wind picked up; the flames beat in the chimney like wings. The sudden noise was a reminder of what they were doing there.

'Should one of us keep lookout?' Sarah Lee suggested.

'Think he'll be early?' Clem asked.

'One of us could wait the other side of the woods,' Johnny said. 'You can see anyone who cuts down off the road from there if there's moonlight. You can hear 'em if there ain't.'

Sarah Lee slipped her watch out of her pocket again.

'Half past eight,' she said. 'We could take an hour each.' She turned to Johnny. 'Unless you want to be on your way.'

'If Clem's staying, I'm staying with him,' Johnny said.

Clem looked uncertain.

Sarah Lee decided. 'We won't hear 'em coming from in here,' she said. 'Johnny, you can cook this second batch. Let them cool off and find a cloth to wrap them in. I'll take the first turn outside.'

She grabbed her jacket from the back of a chair and wound a scarf round her throat.

'If someone comes, I'll hightail it back here. If there ain't time, I'll fire a shot.'

She yanked her hat down and opened the door. The wind roared angrily, seized the ends of her scarf and bent the brim of her hat. It pulled the flames out of the grate and across the stone hearth. She slammed the door after her and shut off the noise of the wind; the flames leapt in the chimney.

Johnny rolled his few clothes in a blanket and packed the biscuits as Sarah Lee had asked.

'When you were losing didn't you want to stop?' Clem asked.

Johnny put down the blanket.

'Couldn't believe it when my losing streak started. I knew I was a better player than them. I could keep a tally in my head of every card that was played; I was sure none of the others could do that.'

'So it was luck?' Clem said.

'I guess.' Johnny shrugged. 'Never won another hand.'

'One day you lost and never won again?' Clem said.

'We've been over this,' Johnny said bitterly. 'I've said I'm sorry.'

Clem shoved a new log on the fire and watched the sparks shower up the chimney.

'Anything else happen on that day?'

Johnny's shoulders slumped; he sat down and stared into the fire.

'Took a walk down the road to ruin and never came back.'

'I meant was there anything different about that day, anything happen that hadn't happened before?'

'I've said I'm sorry.' Johnny stared at him. 'I know it ain't enough but I ain't got nothing else.'

'Anything in the way you played?' Clem pressed him. 'A new deck, maybe?'

'I'm through with talking,' Johnny said. 'I'll wait with you till midnight so you have someone on your side when Jesse James comes. That's all I can do.'

He heaved himself to his feet and looked around for some twine for his blanket roll.

Clem watched him. 'Remember our fishing trips?' he said. 'We'd start out at dawn and leg it down to Bison Creek. We'd sit there all day and not catch a thing. Then when we got back your ma would pretend there was no supper for us because we hadn't done any chores that day.'

Clem smiled to himself.

'First time she did that, I walked right into it. Believed every word.'

Johnny didn't look at him; he concentrated on tying the bedroll.

'She'd taken the Dutch oven off the fire and hidden it round the back of the cabin just to fool us. Remember that?'

Johnny didn't answer.

'We could smell these pies. We knew they were somewhere but we just couldn't find 'em.'

Johnny concentrated on knotting the twine.

'Then she went out back and came in with the oven. Tried to make out one of us had moved it. We still didn't get that the pies were inside until they started to heat through again.'

Clem laughed.

'All along she kept such a poker face, we never realized she was play acting.'

Clem stretched out his legs to feel the warmth of the fire on them.

'Never known anyone for play-acting like your ma.' He smiled at the memory of it all. 'Remember how when we was real small she'd sit us in front of the fire and tell us stories? Not just tell 'em, she'd do all the different voices, pull different faces for each of the characters, walk up and down, waving her arms, acting it all out like she was in a theatre show.'

Johnny threw down the bundle of clothes he'd made.

'What are you telling me this for?' Johnny stared at Clem. 'Why now?'

'I only got good memories of this place,' Clem said. 'Your ma was kind to me when I was a kid. I'll never forget that.'

'I should have left years ago.' Johnny spoke bitterly. 'Just like you did.'

'You know what I went through,' Clem said. 'You know why I ran out.'

'What good did staying do me?' Johnny said. 'I should have gone to Kansas. Rented out the farm and made something of myself in the city.'

'We had some happy times; we should hold on to them,' Clem said. 'That's all I'm saying.'

'What difference has it made?' Johnny said. 'We've both got to clear out now.'

'I used to think of them,' Clem said, 'when I was on my own out there, trailing some lawbreaker, wonderin' if he was going to be waiting for me round the next corner with a gun in his hand.' He stared into the fire. 'When I was under cover in the war, scared to death that someone would stick me with a bayonet every time I fell asleep, I used to think of them then.'

As Clem stared into the fire a woman's face appeared. It watched him for a while, then gradually it twisted in agony. Clem looked away.

'Make yourself remember that you had some good times,' Clem advised. 'Then you'll think you will again.'

'What time is it?' Johnny asked. His face was white; there were shadows under his eyes.

'Ain't got a watch. Sarah Lee won't be long, I guess.'

'When Jesse James shows,' Johnny said, 'you gonna shoot him right off?'

Clem stared into the fire. A man stood there holding a child in his arms.

'Won't have a choice,' Clem said. 'He ain't gonna want to hold a conversation.'

'What do you want me to do?'

Clem looked at him. 'Did you remember to get shells for the shotgun?'

Johnny picked up the blanket roll and checked the knots intently.

'Wouldn't give me credit at the store.'

His voice was barely a whisper.

Outside the wind moaned again; drawn up the chimney, the flames rattled. Johnny looked down at the table where Sarah Lee had been working.

'I ain't baked the biscuits,' he said.

He took the tray and balanced it on the fire, just as Sarah Lee had done.

The door burst open. Johnny wheeled round; Clem went for his gun. The cabin was filled with the sound of the wind thrashing through the trees. Sarah Lee stood there, her shotgun under her arm.

'I've had an idea.'

The men stared at her. Clem holstered his gun.

Sarah Lee shoved the door closed and banished the noise of the wind.

'I'm going to buy this place.'

She looked from one to the other of them.

'Why not?' she continued. 'My pa don't want it. Your pa's only interested in his still.'

On her face there was a big confident grin because she had solved everybody's problems at once.

'The bank will give me a mortgage. I'll put up my horses as collateral; I'll promise them there'll be more coming too. There's good pasture out here; there's a barn. This is where I'll start my breeding ranch.' Sarah Lee spoke quickly; her eyes were bright with excitement. 'Johnny won't have to leave. He can work for me. I wouldn't have no money to pay him at first, of course; he'd have to work for his keep. But that would keep him away from the poker table, wouldn't it?'

She beamed at them.

'And Clem. If you were passing by or you wanted to stop here for a spell, you could stay here too.'

Johnny stared at her.

'I wouldn't have to leave?'

'You could read stories to me in the evenings like you used to. In winter when there was no work to do and the horses were in their stalls in the barn we'd build up a big fire and just sit and take it in turns to read to each other all day.'

Sarah Lee's face was a picture. The words spilled out of her.

'I thought about a way of making extra money too. If there was a horse that was sick, we'd take him in and look after him till he was well. Farmers round here ain't got time to take care of their horses when they're sick. They'd be pleased to have someone do it for them.'

'I could live here?' Johnny repeated.

'Some nights I'd stay over and you'd have to sleep out in the barn,' Sarah Lee said. 'When I wasn't here you could stay in the house, just like you do now. I wouldn't live here all the time because I've still got to take care of my pa.' She was breathless with the excitement of telling them. 'When I was in town, I'd leave you a list of things to do and you'd do 'em before I got back.'

'I would,' Johnny said. 'I'd never let you down.'

A dark, burning smell suddenly filled the cabin. Johnny pulled the tray off the flames, fumbled with the hot biscuits and flipped them over with his fingers to show their blackened undersides.

'There,' he said. 'Just caught 'em.'

Watching him, Sarah Lee's smile tightened.

'Wait,' Clem said suddenly.

He jumped to his feet. He stood stone still and strained to hear something faint and far away; at the same time he slid his gun from its holster.

'What time is it?' he whispered.

Sarah Lee felt for her watch.

'Is there someone in the yard?' Clem said.

No one moved. All they heard was the spit of the fire and the lament of the wind in the trees.

10

Clem motioned to the others to stay back. Sarah Lee raised her shotgun and covered the door; Johnny clung to the wall.

'Shut the door behind me,' Clem hissed.

'No,' Sarah Lee breathed. 'Clem.'

But it was too late. Clem's hand was on the door handle; he kept low and slipped out into the night. The wind roared in the trees; the flames leapt out of the grate. Sarah Lee pushed the door shut and clicked the catch.

Outside, Clem ducked down below the window. The wind was wild. With no moon he could hardly see across the yard. He struggled to make out the shapes of the hen houses and the line of the broken fence.

Two horses were tethered at the rail by the door. Then Clem realized. Two? Was that what he had heard? His own horse and Sarah Lee's appaloosa stood side by side: Johnny's was missing. Someone couldn't have taken her, could they? Was it some kind of trick? Out here, in the swirling darkness, was Jesse

James watching?

The wind carried rain; as he stared into the shadows Clem felt fine droplets against his face. Sometimes he thought he could make out the outline of a horse; sometimes he saw only shadows and empty air. There was only darkness, rain and the sound of the wind crying in the trees. He strained his eyes but it was hopeless.

Clem stepped along the porch, banged on the door and called out. Sarah Lee answered.

As he entered, she lowered her shotgun.

'Horse missing,' Clem said. He looked at Johnny. 'Yours. Didn't you tie him tight?'

Johnny looked confused. How was he supposed to remember?

'Must have been what I heard,' Clem went on. 'Don't reckon there's no one else out there.'

'Can't let her wander off,' Johnny said. 'She won't have gone far.'

He turned up the collar of his jacket, pulled on his hat and headed for the door. Sarah Lee put down her shotgun and shoved another log onto the fire; sparks crackled up the chimney. She started to lift the burnt biscuits off the tray and wrap them in a cloth.

'What time is it?' Clem said.

Sarah Lee produced the watch from her pocket. She glanced at it for a second, then shook it and held it to her ear.

'Stopped,' she said. She shook it again. 'Sometimes it does that.'

'Must be around ten,' Clem said.

'Says eight forty-five,' Sarah Lee said.

She looked down at the roll of clothes Johnny had made.

'What do you think of my idea?'

'You could try. Right now I don't reckon your pa would go for it,' Clem said.

'Why not?' Sarah Lee asked. 'He'd have money in his pocket. Your pa would want that.'

Clem considered. 'The sheriff wants Johnny gone,' he said. 'He ain't going to agree to him staying on out here. Either way, my pa will back him up.'

Sarah Lee picked up Johnny's blanket roll in one hand and the parcel of biscuits in the other.

'Ain't got much, has he?'

'He's got a shotgun,' Clem said. 'That's something.'

'And his books,' Sarah Lee added. 'He'll want to take those.'

The door burst open. Johnny stood there.

'She was in the barn,' he announced. 'Broke free and took shelter from the wind.'

His eye fell on the bundles that Sarah Lee had lined up; the smile went from his face.

'We don't reckon they'd buy it,' Sarah Lee said.

'No?' Johnny looked away from her. 'How much time have we got?'

'Watch ain't workin',' Sarah Lee said.

'You mean you don't know what time it is?'

Panic crossed Johnny's face.

'We should ride into town,' Clem said. 'Sheriff won't let you stay here after midnight. You can catch some shut-eye in the livery and I'll buy you some shotgun shells at the store in the morning.'

'I'll ask 'em about buying the place first,' Sarah Lee said. 'Make it sound like it's easy money for them.'

'They've had their eyes on this place for a long time,' Clem said. 'You got to face that.'

Clem led the way outside. The rain had eased and the wind no longer shook the trees. A cloud uncovered the moon, a few patches of snow remained on the cabin roof and the yard was black with mud. Clem and Sarah Lee mounted up and waited for Johnny to ride his horse out of the barn. When Johnny emerged his collar was up, his hat was low and hid his face.

When they joined the Stoneheart road they rode three abreast, Johnny between Clem and Sarah Lee. Clouds dived across the moon and they were surrounded in darkness; just as quickly the clouds moved and moonlight lit the riders again. Each of them kept their eyes on the road ahead: the direction from which riders would come.

'You never told me,' Clem said, 'how your losing streak started.'

Johnny looked straight ahead, the collar of his saddle jacket high round his face.

'I've been wrong,' he said. 'I caused all this. I gambled the farm away. I let Sarah Lee down. What do you want me to say?'

'I just don't get it,' Clem said. 'You outplay them for a stretch, then everything changes and you never win again.'

'Lady Luck,' Johnny said. 'That's how it happened.'

'You would have thought it would have been win

109

lose, win lose all along.'

'I'm through with it,' Johnny said. 'Don't even want to think about it.'

The three of them rode on in silence for a while. The moon dipped in and out of the clouds; silver light came and went. Once a wolf tracked them for a stretch and kept parallel with them fifty yards off the road. After a while it lost interest and disappeared into the night.

They saw Stoneheart from the top of a rise. The wooden structures looked frail against the dark hills; wisps of smoke from dying fires rose from the chimneys. Dull orange light glowed from one set of windows; a column of woodsmoke rose above the roof. Even from here the riders could tell that this was the saloon.

Would Hackett and Clem's pa be waiting for them? Clem wondered.

'What time do you reckon it is now?' Johnny asked.

Neither of the others answered.

At the edge of town, Clem signalled to the others to let him go first. All the windows were shuttered; mud muffled the sound of their hoofbeats. Up ahead, oil lamps glowed in the saloon window. Fifty yards short, Clem held up his hand to tell them to stop. He slipped out of his saddle and led his horse up the shadowy alley by the store. Sarah Lee and Johnny kept up. Behind the building, they tethered the animals to a hickory bush and followed Clem back down the street.

Approaching the saloon, Clem stopped.

'Whose horse is that?' he hissed.

There were three horses tethered at the rail, Hackett's, Clem's pa's and one they didn't recognize. A cloud slid in front of the moon. The only light they had to go by was the orange glow from the saloon window.

The three of them carried on picking their way over the mud. Up close, they could hear men's voices from inside the saloon. They climbed up onto the wooden porch and peered in at the window.

Hackett was there in his usual place at the table with his back to the stove; Clem's pa sat opposite. Then there was a third man with his back to the door. They could see the outline of his Stetson and his square shoulders. He wore a shirt and dark jacket; his saddle coat was slung over the back of a chair. There were cards, two glasses and an empty bottle on the table; a halo of blue smoke from the sheriff's cigar circled the oil lamps.

Outside, Johnny grasped Clem's arm.

'Is it him? Is it Jesse James?'

'Never set eyes on him,' Clem said. 'Always heard he was a little fella. This guy's tall.'

Just as the mud muffled the sound of their horses' hoofs, it hid the footsteps of the men who approached from the livery stable across the street. The first thing Clem and the others heard was the sounds of the hammer of a Colt being ratcheted back and a Winchester being cocked ready to fire.

Two men stood behind them. The Colt and the Winchester covered them. Clem's hand froze over his gun.

'Wouldn't advise it.' The man with the Colt was stony-eyed. 'Throw down your weapons.'

The two shotguns and Clem's Colt clattered on the boards of the saloon porch. The noise disturbed the men inside. Through the window they saw Hackett and Clem's pa struggle to their feet; the man who had sat with his back to the door turned and drew his Colt in a single motion. A Pinkerton Agency shield was pinned to his jacket; right away Clem recognized Jackson, the agent in charge of the Kearney raid.

The two men shoved Clem and Johnny towards the saloon door and pushed them inside.

Hackett laughed. 'Look who it ain't.'

'Found 'em outside, watching at the window.'

Hackett turned to Jackson. 'You won't be surprised by that. These are the ones I was telling you about.'

'Clem.' Jackson gave a nod of recognition.

'Boss,' Clem said.

'From what the sheriff's been telling me you've got some explaining to do.'

Clem shook his head.

'It's the other way round.'

'See, Mr Jackson,' Hackett fumed. 'Just like I've been saying.'

The two men still had Clem covered.

'All right boys,' Jackson said. 'Back to your posts.' He turned to Johnny. 'Collect up the weapons.'

'What?' Hackett thundered. 'They sneak into town, weapons drawn, after what I've been telling you. Ain't you gonna arrest them?'

Jackson turned to him coldly.

'That's within your jurisdiction, Sheriff; it ain't why we're here.'

Johnny followed the Pinkertons who had brought them in as they headed out into the street.

'You shouldn't have walked out on us, Clem,' Jackson said. 'A Pinkerton should never walk away.'

'What we did was wrong,' Clem said. 'I tried to warn you. You wouldn't listen.'

'He's a coward,' Hackett interrupted. 'Ain't got no loyalty. You can't trust him.'

Johnny came in with the weapons.

'I got no proof of that,' Jackson said.

'Well, I have,' Hackett railed. 'First he runs out on his father, his own kin.'

Jackson stared across the table at Clem's pa, took in his bloodshot eyes, unshaven whiskers and the stink of redeye on his breath.

'Next, he tries to protect this wastrel.' Hackett nodded at Johnny. 'This man has gambled away his farm and everything he owns. On top of that, he carried on a flirtation with my daughter.'

'Pa,' Sarah Lee screamed. Her face was scarlet. She turned to Jackson. 'I don't know you, mister, but I'm telling you that ain't so.'

Jackson held up his hand to show that this was not his business and he wanted no part in it.

'That ain't the worst of it,' Hackett continued. 'I got a theory about this one. I reckon I know why he walked out on that Pinkerton raid.'

'Sheriff,' Jackson protested, 'we ain't got time for theories right now.'

113

He glanced up at the clock above the bar. A quarter to twelve.

'You got to listen,' Hackett said.

'Got to?' Jackson rounded on him. 'You are the sheriff of a one-street farm town. I am the officer in charge of Pinkerton Agents.'

Hackett gripped the edge of the table and his fingers whitened.

'You don't know how things are round here,' he yelled. 'This man is in league with Jesse James.'

Jackson's gun was in his hand and pointed at Clem's chest. Everyone shouted at once. Clem's pa was yelling about treachery and the war; Johnny shouted that everyone who knew Clem trusted him; Sarah Lee screamed at her pa that he was making all this up.

'This is Missouri,' Hackett roared. 'Folks are loyal. Kin matters. This man was a boy when he ran off to join the Pinkertons. He was chasing adventure; he wanted to do right. What young man don't?'

He banged his fist on the table. Glasses skidded onto the floor; the bottle toppled and rolled after them.

'The war made him betray his own people,' Hackett screamed. 'No Missouri man can bear that on his conscience.'

He glared at Jackson.

'You ain't from round here, you don't understand,' Hackett went on. 'Stoneheart may seem like a two-bit town to you, but I am telling you that this man walked out on that operation in Kearney because he'd had enough of what you were doing to Missouri people.

He wanted to help them, didn't he? He didn't want you to burn them out? He tried to stop you.'

Jackson's Colt was still pointed at Clem's ribs.

'It is my belief,' Hackett thundered, 'that this man aims to assist Jesse James when he gets here tonight.'

Appearing not to look at him, Clem watched the Pinkerton man's reaction in the mirror behind the bar. As Jackson thumbed back the hammer on his Colt, Clem dived for the empty bottle that had rolled onto the floor, snatched it up and flung it.

The bottle curled through the air, caught Jackson's wrist. The Colt fired wide before it was knocked out of his hand and skidded across the floor. Everyone shouted. Clem's pa tipped his chair over backwards and crashed onto the floor; Hackett made a grab for Clem as he leapt to his feet.

The saloon door crashed back on its hinges. The two agents stood there with their weapons drawn. Jackson clutched his wrist to stop the lancing pain; agony twisted his face. He flung himself back against the bar.

'What are you waiting for?' he yelled. 'Shoot him.'

11

Sarah Lee leapt in front of the Pinkertons with her arms outstretched. The men yelled and tried to push her aside. Johnny made a dive for Jackson's gun, which spun to the floor. Hackett staggered and went for his gun, but he was slow: he was wrong-footed by Sarah Lee's facing the agents' guns.

'No, not her,' Hackett's voice wavered.

Clem's pa struggled to his feet. White-faced, Jackson clutched his swollen wrist. As the agents stood there with the confusion confronting them, they hesitated.

It was long enough. Clem jabbed the barrel of his Colt against Jackson's temple. Pain sapped Jackson's strength; his face was the colour of snow. He slumped helplessly against the bar.

'Put your guns away,' Clem snapped.

The agents looked from one to the other, then did as he said.

'These are Pinkertons on the trail of a wanted

outlaw,' Hackett blustered. 'What do you think you're doing?'

Clem swung his Colt towards Hackett.

Hackett raised his hands and looked to the others for support. Clem thumbed back the hammer of his Colt.

Hackett didn't hesitate: he laid his .45 on the table. Clem snatched the gun, shoved it in his belt and turned to the Pinkertons.

'You fellas get back to your positions.'

'I could have you arrested right now,' Jackson gasped. He clutched his wrist and sat back, weak with pain. 'Feels like you've broke my hand.'

'I'm on your side,' Clem said. 'The sheriff is spinning you a line.'

'You in charge now?' Hackett jeered.

Sarah Lee gently slipped her arm under Jackson's shoulder and helped him to his feet.

'I'll strap up his arm,' she said.

She took his weight and led him towards the storeroom behind the bar. Jackson screwed up his face against the pain.

With Jackson gone, Hackett and Clem's pa sat back down in their usual places round the card table. Johnny stood by the door; he still held Jackson's Colt.

'You can't let me wait for Jesse James with no weapon,' Hackett said.

'I ain't armed neither,' Clem's pa chimed in.

The black Roman numerals of the clock above the bar showed five minutes to midnight.

'Safer if you ain't,' Clem said. 'We'll sit here and

wait for him. The agents across the street will follow him in.'

'I want my weapon,' Hackett said.

'You think you can outdraw Jesse James?' Clem said. 'I want you to change seats.'

'What?'

'You heard me.' Clem waved his pistol at the opposite chair. 'And you.'

He indicated that his pa should move out of his seat to the one with its back to the door.

'What is this?' Hackett said.

'Do what he says,' Johnny told him. He pulled back the hammer on Hackett's Colt.

'You ain't about to shoot nobody.' Hackett stood up. 'You ain't got it in you.' He glared at Clem. 'I don't know what you're playing at.'

'Poker,' Clem said.

He reached down, opened the trap to the stove and shoved in another log.

'When Jesse James comes, I want him to see a poker game.'

Clem's pa suddenly understood. 'The Pinks in the stable will come across and shoot him in the back.'

'We should be armed,' Hackett said. 'And why are we having to move places?'

'Shut up and sit down,' Clem said. 'If there's trouble, the first one Jesse James will go for is the one who's packing.'

Clem took Hackett's usual seat with its back to the stove.

'See why I like that place now the stove's going,'

Hackett said.

'Johnny, get your jacket off and stand behind the bar,' Clem said. 'Put the guns out of sight.'

'Let me have my Colt,' Hackett fumed. 'This is foolishness.'

Clem ignored him again.

'Cards?'

Hackett felt in his vest pocket and produced a greasy deck.

'Deal,' Clem said.

Hackett riffled the cards and shuffled them hand to hand.

He lowered his hands onto the table.

'You actually want us to play?'

Clem nodded.

Johnny took a bottle of rye and a handful of glasses from the shelf and set them on the bar.

'You gonna pour us a shot?' Clem's pa said.

'No,' Clem said. 'You may need to move fast.'

Hackett shuffled again, then dealt.

They played the hand quickly, watching each other over the tops of their cards. Over Hackett's shoulder, Clem kept an eye on the saloon door. Behind the bar, Johnny rolled up his sleeves and made a show of polishing the glasses. Over his head the minute hand moved past midnight.

Hackett won; Clem played badly; Clem's pa was aware that he had his back to the door and couldn't concentrate. Hackett took a stogie out of his pocket, lit it and dealt again. Gradually, Clem's pa was drawn into the play. Clem took barely any notice of his cards

119

and let the men believe he was losing because he had no grasp of the game.

If anyone had walked into the saloon, the scene would have convinced them. The bartender calmly polished glasses; the players were intent on their game. Blue cigar smoke hung round the oil lamps and the fire crackled in the stove.

Hackett won every hand. After the third, when it was his turn to deal again, he put down the cards and stared at Clem.

'How much longer are we going to keep this up?'

The glasses chinked together as Johnny arranged them on the bar. The clock showed half past midnight.

'Could do with a drink,' Clem's pa chimed.

Sarah Lee led Jackson out from the back room. His face was still ashen; his eyes narrowed with pain. Sarah Lee had made splints for his wrist out of pieces of a packing case and bound them tight with strips of his shirt tail, then she'd strapped his arm across his chest.

'Reckon he's got a fracture,' Sarah Lee said.

'You shouldn't be out here,' Hackett snapped. 'You won't even be able to get out of the way.'

Suddenly all their attention refocused on Jesse James's arrival, as if a cold draught had knifed across the warm room.

'I'm stayin',' Jackson snarled. 'This is my operation.'

'You Pinkertons,' Hackett said. 'Think you can walk in anywhere and take over.'

'We ain't got no weapons,' Clem's pa added.

Jackson sat up in his chair. The movement caused him a stab of pain.

'You want these men to face Jesse James unarmed?' Jackson said. 'Pass the sheriff his sidearm.'

'I want them to play cards,' Clem said. 'The agents across the street will do the rest.'

He slid Hackett's pistol to him across the table.

Hackett holstered the gun and dealt again. Sarah Lee went and stood by Johnny behind the bar.

'He's late,' Hackett said. 'What's keeping him?'

'Think he runs to a timetable?' Jackson scoffed. 'When you've been tracking Jesse James as long as I have, you know that most of it is guesswork. Usually we arrive after he's long gone. Makes a change to be in a place ahead of him.'

'Know what he looks like?' Hackett said.

'Never seen him,' Jackson said. 'He keeps himself hid.'

'Read the letters he writes to the newspaper?'

Jackson scowled.

'You mean where he says he never shot that cashier?'

'Said he wouldn't hand himself in because he reckoned he wouldn't get a fair trial,' Clem's pa said.

Jackson snorted.

'Lot of people down here believe him,' Hackett said.

'Lot of people down here know where he is and won't say,' Jackson said. He looked nervously towards the door as if he had said too much.

Hackett considered his cards.

'He shot a child in Kansas,' Jackson said. 'A girl. Hear about that?'

'He wrote a letter to the *Weekly Times* about it,' Clem's pa said. 'It was an accident. He offered to send money to the parents to pay for the medical bills.'

'That makes it right?' Jackson sneered. 'What's he gonna pay them with? Money he stole from the bank?'

Hackett won the hand again. He looked over at Clem.

'Ain't much of a card player, are you?'

'Never spent much time playing,' Clem said.

'Seems to me,' Hackett said slowly, 'you might like to try a hand of solitaire.'

He looked at Clem.

'After all, you're the one Jesse James wants. Ain't much point in the rest of us being here. You could lay out a solitaire hand; the Pinkerton boys would be across the street.'

He squared up the cards and passed them to Clem's pa to shuffle.

'Or don't you want to face him on your own?'

'You'd be the ones who were running out,' Clem said.

'What time is it?' Hackett leaned back in his chair to catch sight of the saloon clock.

'Fifteen minutes to one,' Johnny said.

'He ain't coming,' Clem's pa said. 'I know that Kearney road. It wouldn't have taken him this long.'

'He'll come,' Jackson said. 'Besides money, the one thing Jesse James is interested in is revenge. If he's heard the Pinkertons who raided his house are here, he'll show up.'

Clem's pa looked up from his cards.

'Can't hardly blame him for that,' he said.

'Know why he shot that cashier?' Jackson snapped. 'Claimed it was payback for a guy he rode with who got killed in the war.'

Clem's pa stared at him.

'He got the wrong man,' Jackson said. 'James is a thief and a murderer. This talk of revenge is a cover-up.'

The men studied their cards. Once again Clem made blunders, which surprised the others and made them smile.

'I think we should play for money,' Hackett said.

Clem's pa grunted agreement.

'You forgot why we're here?' Jackson said. 'Keep playing and just make sure you keep your wits about you.'

Hackett turned towards the door.

'He could be outside right now.'

Everyone kept still. Johnny put down his cloth and ran his fingers over the steel barrel of the Colt on the shelf underneath the bar. When Hackett ground out the butt of his stogie under his boot heel, the noise caught everyone's attention and they turned towards him.

'Know where Frank and Jesse learned to sneak up on people in the night?' Jackson said.

Hackett looked at him.

'When they was with Quantrill in the war,' Jackson said. 'That's where they got a taste of taking what

123

wasn't theirs, killing for it too.'

'What are you telling us this for?' Hackett said. 'Everyone round here knows who Quantrill was.'

'I was just saying,' Jackson said, 'if Jesse James can sneak up and surprise us in the dark, he learned how to do that fighting for the Confederacy.'

Hackett's face darkened.

'If you had done your job we wouldn't be in this mess.'

'All right,' Clem broke in. 'I'll go outside and take a look around. When I come back, we'll play for money.'

'My agents will shoot anyone who passes through that door,' Jackson said. 'They won't be able to make out who it is in the dark.'

Clem put down his cards and stood up.

'I'll go out the back way.'

Clem caught Sarah Lee's eye as he headed for the storeroom behind the saloon. Her hand rested on the shotgun on the shelf under the bar.

Outside, the street was empty and quiet. Wind moved the clouds and the town was washed in silver light.

Rather than attract the attention of the Pinkertons holed up in the livery, Clem doubled back and made his way down the street behind the buildings. With his Colt ready in his hand, he trod quietly. Apart from a lamp burning in the window at the back of the store, there was nothing, just emptiness, shadows and silence.

Clem played up and down these alleys as a kid. They

had seemed as wide as highways to him then; now they were cramped spaces, barely wide enough for two men to pass. He remembered how he and Johnny, exhausted from playing chase, would lie in wait for each other round the corners of the buildings and leap out with a terrifying scream when one or the other approached. He recalled how women would rush out of the store, imagining some terrible accident. He and Johnny would run away laughing in the sunshine.

By the store wall Clem pulled his coat tighter and scanned the street. Still nothing. A muddy avenue ran under the moonlight one direction; a muddy trail ran out of town in the other. This was the road along which a rider from Kearney would come.

What about the Pinkertons in the livery stable? Shouldn't he check with them that they hadn't seen anything? Being out here in the silence for this long would have made them jumpy. If he called out, would they shoot?

Clem could hear someone moving around as he passed the back room of the store; Passmore was having a sleepless night. The dull glow from an oil lamp lit the window.

Crates and wooden packing-cases were stacked untidily along the wall. A cloud slid in front of the moon and all light disappeared. Clem instinctively grabbed the edge of a crate. For a second he felt it sway under his grasp, then the pile of crates clattered over him. Knowing the Pinkertons were inclined to shoot before they asked questions, Clem's first thought was: had they heard it?

In the darkness, as Clem struggled over the boxes to get away, he tripped, slipped, fell and brought down more cases with him. As he picked himself up the light in the back room of the store went out. He heard the rattle of the sash being drawn up.

'That you, Jesse James?' Passmore roared. 'You trying to rob my store?'

Clem's protest was smothered in the blast from Passmore's shotgun.

Pain seared Clem's shoulder as stray shot caught him; he fell back into the heap of crates. Passmore carried on shouting. Clem heard him break open the gun. He yelled to him not to shoot but Passmore was yelling to keep his courage up as he struggled to reload.

'Think you can come here and break into my store?' Passmore's voice was high and frightened. 'You better think again, mister.'

Bruised and shaken, Clem shoved the packing cases aside. His boots slipped on the wet wood and slid on the muddy ground. He had nothing to support him and crashed face forward again. With a triumphant yell, Passmore loosed off another barrel.

12

'It's me,' Clem yelled.

He threw aside the crates and pallets which were heaped on top of him; splinters tore his fingers, and his back and shoulders ached with bruises. He heard Passmore reload.

Clem yelled again as he stumbled to his feet.

'Who?' the old man answered.

'There's no one here,' Clem said. 'I've checked along the street.'

'Ain't slept a wink,' Passmore said. 'Been keeping watch all night.'

Clem waved to Passmore, picked his way through the pile of crates and headed back to the saloon. Aware that everyone in town now knew where he was, he stepped quickly in and out of the shadows between the buildings.

The back door to the saloon storeroom was ajar, just as Clem had left it. He hallooed but there was no answer. The store was dark; orange light from the oil lamps showed round the edge of the door to the saloon. Clem called again, softly this time, as he opened the door.

The saloon was empty. There was light from the oil lamps, warmth from the fire and the lingering smell of tobacco, that was all.

Clem slipped his gun out of its holster and scanned the room. Chairs were pushed aside and a fresh bottle of redeye stood on the table at which everyone had sat; clean glasses were lined up on the bar. Everything else was the same. The door was closed; the window glass shone like jet and reflected the room inside.

A small reflection of movement in the mirror behind the bar caught Clem's eye. He leapt forward, ready to dive out of the way, his finger tight on the trigger of his .45. Leaning against the bar, trussed like chickens ready for the pot, were Hackett and Clem's pa. Their wrists were tied behind them to their ankles; neckerchiefs gagged their mouths.

Crimson-faced, Hackett tugged at the ropes that held him; the kerchief muffled whatever it was he was trying to say. Clem's pa was slumped against him; the edges of his mouth were blue and his eyes were closed. A line of dark blood ran down his neck from the back of his head and soaked into the collar of his shirt.

Clem checked the rest of the room, the corners, behind the bar; there was no one else there. He knelt down, unsheathed his hunting knife and cut Hackett loose. Hackett yanked the kerchief away from his mouth and pulled himself from under Clem's pa. He toppled and his skull thudded against the floor.

'Should have shot him,' Hackett snarled. 'Should

have drilled him, the first chance I got. What did you let him have a gun for?'

Clem sawed at the ropes which trussed his pa. The old man groaned; his eyes flicked open briefly.

'Even Sarah Lee tried to make him stop,' Hackett went on. 'Held a gun in my face. When your pa objected he slugged him.'

'What are you talking about?' Clem said. 'Where's Jackson?'

'Went to check on his Pinkerton boys.' Hackett spat. 'Left right after you did. That's when he jumped us.'

'Johnny did this?' Clem struggled to understand.

There was a thumping noise behind the bar, a repeated knocking as if someone insisted on being let in. Clem's hand flew to his gun.

'Threw her in the store cupboard,' Hackett said.

'Clem.' It was Sarah Lee's muffled voice.

Clem climbed over the bar and pulled away the stool which was wedged under the store cupboard handle. Sarah Lee burst through the door.

'Couldn't stop him,' she sobbed. 'Said he's going to shoot Jesse James and claim the reward.'

'I'd go after him, but he's got my gun,' Hackett said quickly.

'He says he knows the reason for it all,' Sarah Lee went on. 'The reward will give him a stake for one last play.'

'Johnny?' Clem said. 'Gone out there after Jesse James?'

'Sarah Lee,' Hackett barked, 'I want your shotgun.'

'He left it for me,' Sarah Lee said. 'Said it was in case I needed it.'

'Give it to me right now.' Hackett thrust out his hand.

'Did you hear her?' Clem snapped. 'He left it for her.'

'Next time I see that no-good,' Hackett blustered, 'I swear—'

'Sit back down,' Clem said.

He gestured to the seats by the stove, helped his pa over to one and turned to Sarah Lee.

'That shotgun is yours. Don't let him near it.'

'That man's a coward. He slugged your pa and stole my weapon,' Hackett fumed. 'What are you protecting him for? If he was here, I'd shoot him right now.'

'Coward?' Clem said. 'He's the one out there looking for Jesse James.'

'I'm sheriff,' Hackett said. 'You expect me to stay here without a gun when my own daughter's armed?'

'Shut up,' Clem said.

Clem's pa came to enough to focus on the whiskey bottle in front of him and poured himself a drink; the parchment colour was disappearing from his face. Sarah Lee leaned over the bar and picked up the shotgun.

'How long's he been gone?' Clem said.

'No time,' Sarah Lee said. 'Jackson left right after you; he went right after Jackson.'

Clem considered. 'Reckons he's going to use the reward as a stake?'

'Said something about knowing how it had happened. Couldn't figure what he meant.' Sarah Lee's face was pale. Her grip tightened on the shotgun. 'We heard some shooting. Reckoned you'd run into trouble. That's when he went out. Said he was going to help you. Said he'd claim the reward at the same time.'

'We thought Jesse James had got you,' Hackett sneered. 'That was a shotgun we heard, not your .45.'

'Passmore,' Clem said. 'Down at the store. He's been sitting up all night.'

'That old fool after the reward too?' Hackett scoffed.

They looked at the sheets of jet glass and the reflections of themselves, suddenly aware that this was what anyone outside would see. Clem led Sarah Lee to a table at the side of the saloon by the stove; they sat with their backs to the wall. Sarah Lee rested the shotgun across her knees; Clem's Colt was in his hand. Their eyes never left the door.

Clem's pa poured himself another drink. 'All of us should be entitled to a share of the reward,' he said. 'We've all been here waiting. We're all part of the trap.'

No one answered him. Hackett took out his watch and checked the time.

'Reckon Johnny will …' Sarah Lee began.

Clem looked at her.

'Still black as pitch out there,' Hackett said. 'Still a few hours till sunup.'

He kicked the catch and swung the stove door open. The fire rattled in the chimney. Hackett reached down, shoved in another log and clanged the door shut. He took a fresh stogie out of his vest pocket and lit it, leaned back and picked up the deck of cards.

'Don't suppose nobody wants a game?'

No one answered. Clem's pa gulped his whiskey; Clem and Sarah Lee kept their eyes on the door. Their bones ached with fatigue; the idea of staging another poker game was too much.

What had Johnny meant? Clem wondered. *He knew how it happened.* How *what* happened?

Clem watched Hackett shuffle and reshuffle. Sour-faced, he concentrated on the deck. Clem pictured him standing in their yard years before, the day his ma sat with her back to the window. Younger then of course, thinner and lithe in his movements but even then Hackett had had that same unsmiling face.

One quick glance at his pa and Clem saw an old whiskey-sodden farmer. His eyes were salmon-rimmed and watery; his fleshy face was red with rye. Clem remembered him on that day too, standing in the yard holding a smile on his mouth to show the sheriff that what had happened didn't bother him at all.

Clem's ma had been inside the cabin. He remembered the noise of her scraping the chairs across the wooden floor; she couldn't come out to talk to the men because it was the day she had spring cleaning to do.

Then there was Sarah Lee. Even though she had put up with years of her pa's boorish criticism, she still skivvied for him just as she had done every day when she got home from the schoolhouse. It was an aching disappointment for her that Johnny could have made

132

a better life for her, but had turned out not to be strong enough. Her solace was her appaloosas.

And Johnny. Now he was out there searching for the most dangerous man in the state, heedless of the risk to himself, reckless of the danger to the others.

Everything was different, Clem thought, but nothing had changed. His pa drank; Hackett bullied; Sarah Lee made do; Johnny dreamed.

The door exploded open. Johnny was hurled across the floor. The two Pinkertons followed him in; Jackson strode after them.

'Found this fool in the middle of the street,' Jackson sneered. 'Claimed he was looking for Jesse James.'

Johnny groaned and levered himself up.

'Don't you know we could have shot you?' Jackson went on. 'What use would reward money be to you then?'

'Should have shot him and had done with it,' Hackett said. 'He ain't no use to his own shadow.'

'Pa.' Sarah Lee sat up straight.

Johnny leaned against the side of the bar and brushed the dust off his clothes.

'Don't you realize that if Jesse James saw you wandering around in the dark, he would have guessed we were waiting for him?' Jackson glared at him. His wrist was still bandaged tight; pain drew the strength out of him. He found a chair near the door.

'If he was out there and he saw you, he's probably hightailed it by now.' Jackson rammed the point home. 'That's most likely what's happened.'

'He wasn't,' Johnny said. 'Didn't see nothing, didn't hear nothing.'

Jackson waved his words away as though Johnny didn't understand and he couldn't be bothered to explain.

'He was doing his best,' Sarah Lee spoke up. 'If he had found Jesse James, it would have saved you a whole lot of trouble.'

'We're professionals, ma'am.' Jackson touched the brim of his hat. 'If anyone's going to track him down we will.'

'Well, you ain't done much of a job of it so far.' Hackett laughed. 'I ain't saying no more than that.'

'We'll get him.' Jackson scowled. 'This kind of thing takes time.'

He nodded to the two agents.

'Best get back to your posts. If he doesn't show by first light, we'll call this off.'

The agents slipped out of the door into the street. Jackson turned to Johnny.

'Stay in here, understand? You're lucky you ain't crowbait.'

'What time is it?' Johnny said.

Jackson looked up at the clock.

'Just after three.'

'First light's at five,' Clem's pa said.

His hand reached for the bottle again.

134

13

When watery yellow light broke the darkness in the east, only Clem was awake. Sarah Lee sat beside him resting on his shoulder. His pa snored gently with his head on the table; Hackett had his feet up on a chair; Johnny sat on the floor and leaned back against the bar. Jackson had crossed the street to be with the agents in the livery stable an hour before.

The oil lamps had died; there was a chill in the room. Sarah Lee woke as Clem prised himself out of his chair and went to see to the fire.

'Maybe the Pinkertons got it wrong,' Sarah Lee said, relief in her voice.

Clem riddled the stove and waited for the flames to catch again. The others stirred but didn't wake.

'I'll fix some coffee.' Sarah Lee stepped over Johnny's spread eagled legs. She found the percolator and coffee in the cupboard behind the bar. When the fire was blazing, Clem crossed over to the window.

Jackson and the two agents led their horses out of the stable already saddled up and ready to ride.

Jackson's arm was still bandaged tight to his chest. He was giving orders to the men. He saw Clem watching him and waved. The three of them started across the street to the saloon. The sound of the door opening woke the others. The men headed for the stove and held their hands over it.

'We'll be moving out,' Jackson said. 'There may be a wire waiting for me at Liberty. If there ain't, we'll hightail it to Kansas. At least we know Frank was headed there.'

The lid of the percolator clattered and the smell of coffee filled the room.

Jackson turned to Clem. 'You know there'll be more killing,' he said. 'Till he's behind bars. Four men would be more effective than three, especially since. . . .'

He glanced down at his arm.

Clem shook his head. 'I come from this place. Ain't ready to leave yet.'

'You want to stay here?' Jackson said.

There was surprise in his voice. He looked around at the others. Clem's pa was rubbing his eyes; Hackett barged between the agents for a place at the stove; Sarah Lee lined up the coffee cups on the bar. Outside, thin light rose through the sky; mud from the street clung to the legs of the horses and ruined their feathering.

'We need good men,' Jackson insisted.

'After Kearney—' Clem began.

'You know that wasn't intended,' Jackson said.

'Your intelligence was wrong,' Clem said. 'Look

136

what happened.'

Jackson stared out into the street.

'You want us to let Jesse James go free because of that?'

Grey daylight pushed the shadows into the corners of the room. Clem's pa upended the bottle of redeye over his coffee, Hackett hogged the heat from the stove. Johnny leaned against the bar.

'There's been thieving going on,' Clem explained. 'I want you to help me do something about it.'

'Thieving's everywhere,' Jackson said. 'There's only one Jesse James and we're on his trail.'

Clem walked into the centre of the room with his coffee cup in his hand.

'Sheriff?'

Hackett turned from the stove and scowled at him.

'Thought we might play a hand of cards before these fellas are on their way,' Clem said.

'You've had all night to play cards,' Hackett snapped.

'Deal him in.' Clem nodded to Jackson.

'Me?' Jackson said.

'Clem.' Sarah Lee stood beside him. 'What are you doing?'

Clem took his Colt from his holster and covered them.

Hackett jumped back.

'Sit down, Sheriff.' Clem pointed to the seat with its back to the bar.

'Are you crazy?' Hackett said.

Clem turned to Jackson.

'Now you. I asked you to help me.' He waved his Colt at the opposite chair.

The agents' hands were on their sidearms.

'What is this?' Hackett fumed.

'Deal,' Clem said.

He thumbed back the hammer on his Colt. The agents moved towards him. Jackson held up his good hand to warn them off.

'I ain't. . . .' Hackett blustered.

From the sheriff's usual seat with its back to the stove, Jackson looked round the room. A smile spread across his face.

'Do as he says,' Jackson said.

Hackett slipped a deck out of his vest pocket and set it down on the table. He turned to Clem.

'This is ridiculous,' he protested.

Jackson leaned across the table, fixed his eyes on Hackett and spoke sharply.

'Deal.'

Hackett shuffled the deck and dealt. They picked up their cards. Clem's pa looked over to the bar as if he expected another bottle to be there. Jackson leaned back and looked at Clem.

'Don't need to go no further,' he said. 'You made your point.'

He put his cards face down on the table. Hackett studied his hand.

'Mirror behind the bar.' Jackson laughed. 'I can see your hand, Sheriff. You've already lost.'

Johnny stepped closer to the table. Hackett looked up as though he had been so intent on his hand that he had only just realized they were talking.

'What?'

'Anyone who sits here can see your hand,' Jackson said.

Colour rose in Hackett's face.

'What are you saying?'

Jackson shrugged. 'That's all I'm saying.'

'Sheriff always sits where you are.' Johnny appealed to Clem. 'Won't let nobody else sit there.'

Jackson pushed back his chair and stood up.

'Was that what you were trying to show me?'

'Sheriff's cheated you out of your farm, Johnny; my pa's helped him. They've stolen away everything you own,' Clem said. 'You were too wrapped up in remembering all the cards and calculating the odds to see it.'

Hackett appeared to study his cards.

'So?' Jackson said.

'I want you to arrest him,' Clem said. 'My pa's in on it. Him too.'

Hackett squared up the deck and placed it neatly in the centre of the table. He looked up at Clem. A sneer touched the corners of his mouth. Clem's pa pushed his chair back from the table and looked contemptuously at his son as if this was no more than he'd expected.

'There was somebody cheating in every saloon in the whole of Missouri last night,' Jackson said. 'You forgotten why we're here?'

Jackson sat back in his chair.

'I've been holding on to my temper,' Hackett breathed. His words were little bullets, hard and deliberate. 'Ain't many men would put up with these kind

139

of accusations.'

'That's right.' Clem's pa encouraged him.

'When the sheriff of a town is accused of cheating, you'd think there would be some mention of witnesses,' Hackett said. 'Some talk of proof.'

Clem turned to Jackson.

'I've shown you how he's done it.'

Johnny said nothing; his eyes burned into Hackett's face. Hackett looked through him and spoke to Jackson.

'This is what you expect from a fella who runs out on his own family to join the Pinkertons,' Hackett said. 'Then he runs out on the Pinkertons when they're on the trail of Jesse James himself.'

He leaned back in his chair and invited Jackson to take this in.

'I ain't got time for this,' Jackson snapped.

He gestured to the two agents to head towards the door.

'This is a local dispute,' Jackson went on. 'You want this settled, someone best call in a marshal from Kansas.'

He glared at Clem.

'You know this ain't Pinkerton business.'

'Jesse James's trail has gone cold,' Clem said. 'Wrong's been done here. . . .'

'I'll be the judge of whether we've lost Jesse James,' Jackson said. 'Like I said, this ain't Pinkerton business. Anyhow, the sheriff's right. There's no evidence.'

Clem's pa laughed. A gargle in his throat turned into an explosion of coughing; his face boiled.

Hackett felt for a stogie in his vest pocket; his thin lips twitched into a smile.

The agents pushed open the saloon door. Jackson followed.

'Wait.' Sarah Lee stepped out from behind the bar. 'There's something else.'

Jackson turned towards her.

'I want to report a murder.'

Sarah Lee's face was pale; her voice shook. Jackson looked at her as if he was trying to make up his mind about something.

'He did it.' Sarah Lee pointed at Clem's pa. 'My pa knew about it and he kept quiet. They both covered it up.'

'What?' Clem's pa shoved his chair back from the table.

'Are you crazy?' Hackett was on his feet.

'It was years ago,' Sarah Lee said. 'A guy came through looking for work. Clem's pa beat him to death and buried the body in the woods out at his farm.'

'Years ago?' Jackson struggled to understand. 'How do you know this?'

'I heard my pa telling the story,' Sarah Lee said. 'I heard him laughing.'

'What are you talking about?' Hackett yelled. 'Don't listen to her.'

'This is foolishness,' Clem's pa growled. His face burned.

Jackson hesitated.

'It's true.' Sarah Lee twisted her hands together

141

until her fingers were a knot. 'He said no one would ever find the body.'

'When was this?' Jackson said.

'I don't know,' Sarah Lee said. 'I was a kid.'

'A kid?' Jackson echoed.

Hackett lit his stogie and blew a column of smoke into the room. Clem's pa laughed until a fit of coughing clamped his chest.

'I don't know when,' Sarah Lee said. 'I was young.' The she added defiantly, 'I know what I heard.'

Clem's thoughts somersaulted. Pieces were missing from the jigsaw puzzle in his head. He remembered the drifter in the yard, with his pa standing over him. He remembered his ma in the cabin with her back to the window; her hands were over her ears and her eyes were closed. He saw Hackett standing there talking to his pa.

'She's right,' Clem said. 'Something happened back then. We could ride out to the farm and take a look.'

'You people,' Jackson thundered. 'First you expect me to arrest the sheriff for cheating at cards, then you want me to look for a body in the woods that might have been put there ten years ago.'

Clem's pa recovered from coughing; a grin was slapped across his red face.

'If something's wrong,' Clem said simply, 'you should put it right.'

'I am on the trail of Jesse James,' Hackett said. 'You should be riding with me.'

He turned up the collar of his coat and strode towards the door.

Clem stood at the window of the saloon and watched the Pinkertons ride out. Their horses kicked up black mud from the street.

It was too much to ask, Clem thought. Jackson was an agency man through and through. If there was a plan he would follow it; if there was an agreement he would stick to it. Clem remembered the cabin at Kearney. Jackson wouldn't deviate from what they had decided to do; the fact that no one had checked to see who was inside was irrelevant. Jackson had kept to his plan.

Clem turned his back on the window and faced into the saloon. Sarah Lee and Johnny were standing by the bar. Sarah Lee was ashen-faced; she laced and unlaced her fingers. Johnny looked shocked, the strength which he had regained since they found him shivering on the prairie was gone. He seemed hardly aware of where he was.

Clem's pa was slumped in his chair at the poker table. He stared at Clem with loathing, his lips were a scar in his florid face. His breathing was awkward, a cough rattled in his chest.

Hackett stood by the stove. His coat was pushed back and showed the .45 in his belt. He scowled at Clem, glanced contemptuously at Johnny and ignored Sarah Lee. The morning light caught the sheriff's star pinned to his lapel. He drew on his stogie and flicked the ash onto the floor.

'You know what would have happened in the old days?' Hackett began. 'Someone made accusations like that they would have been shot before they had

143

time to turn round.'

Clem stared at him. 'What are you saying?'

'I'm telling you to leave town,' Hackett said. 'You ran out on us once. You can do it again right now.'

'If he leaves,' Sarah Lee said, 'I'm going with him.'

'You ain't going nowhere.' Hackett rounded on her. 'I don't want to hear your voice after what you said. The Pinkertons didn't take no notice of you so why should I?'

Clem's pa coughed agreement.

'What Sarah Lee said was true, wasn't it?' Clem stared at his pa. 'About the drifter.'

A gutteral cough buckled the old man's chest; he fought for breath.

'Sheriff's right,' he said. 'You ran out on me. Now you've run out on the Pinkertons.'

'This is my fault,' Johnny said suddenly. 'I should have realized what you two were doing. You did this week on week until I had nothing left.'

His face hardened.

'I'm calling you out, Sheriff. You can face me in the street right now. You stole my farm and everything I've got.'

'Johnny,' Sarah Lee gasped. She grabbed his arm but he shook her off.

Clem stepped towards him but Johnny barged past him and made for the door.

'No,' Sarah Lee shouted.

The cough which tore at Clem's pa's chest turned into raucous, violent laughter.

14

Hackett grabbed Sarah Lee's arm.

'Go back home,' he snarled. 'Make breakfast.'

He frogmarched her through the saloon door; Johnny was ahead of them. At the bottom of the porch steps Hackett shoved her in the direction of the sheriff's office.

'I've told you. Stay away from him.' Sarah Lee ran up the steps again before Hackett could grab her.

Red sunlight bled into the watery sky. Johnny was waiting for the sheriff.

'Sure you want to go through with this?' Hackett called.

He glanced back at the saloon porch; Clem and his pa were watching. There was a smirk on Hackett's mouth and a look on his face which said *I gave him a chance but he didn't take it.*

Johnny's face was pale; his eyes stared; his right hand which hung near the Colt in his belt shook slightly. There was a moment where time stretched as the men looked at each other. Neither spoke. They took in the distance between them, each judged the height of the other and stared at the place on the chest where he would aim. Hackett noticed Johnny's trembling hand.

During this long moment the men on the porch were still; they knew what was going to happen. Time stopped. They watched Johnny and Hackett face each other, caught between the red sky and the black mud. There was nothing they could do except wait for time to start again.

Sarah Lee burst out of the saloon, the shotgun in her hands. She elbowed her way between Clem and his pa and loosed off one of the barrels over their heads, so close that they reeled back.

'Stop this,' she screamed. 'Right now.'

Hackett and Johnny gaped at her; shock emptied their faces.

Clem's pa grabbed the barrel of the shotgun in his big farmer's hand. He swung a fist and broke Sarah Lee's nose. Blood exploded over her face. Her grip on the shotgun melted and he wrenched it out of her grasp. Sarah Lee staggered back, her hands over her face to hold back the blood.

Clem yelled and reached for the shotgun. His pa swung it on him and jabbed him in the belly.

'Stay back,' his pa yelled. 'I got one more barrel.'

Sarah Lee was bent double. Pain rang in her head; her bloody fingers caged her face.

Hackett turned back to Johnny.

'They can't save you,' Hackett said. 'Count of three?'

Above them on the porch Sarah Lee screamed. She

146

launched herself at the shotgun barrel; Clem's pa held the gun like a vice. Clem was shouting now. His arm was round his pa's thick neck and wrenched his head back. The old man's grip on the gun was steel; he fell back against Clem with his full weight and smashed him into the saloon wall.

The second barrel of the shotgun blasted. Shot tore away the shoulder of Sarah Lee's buckskin jacket, ripped her shirt and flayed the skin. She let go her hold on the barrel and staggered backwards; Clem's pa fell. The shotgun clattered onto the wooden floor of the porch.

'Sarah Lee,' Johnny yelled.

He made a dash for the porch where Sarah Lee had fallen. She called something to him but her words were lost. Johnny had barely taken a single pace before Hackett fired; the shot echoed between the buildings and under the red dawn sky. Shooting from the hip at a moving target, Hackett's aim was high. Johnny's body lurched as the bullet smashed through his shoulder. He doubled over and fell.

Clem shoved his pa away and struggled to his feet; his Colt was in his hand. Hackett stared up at Clem on the porch; with a deliberate motion he holstered his gun and held his arms wide.

'He called me out,' Hackett said.

Clem levelled his Colt at Hackett.

'You stole everything he had,' Clem said. 'Even tried to keep Sarah Lee away from him.'

Pausing on every step to take her weight, Sarah Lee carefully made her way down from the porch. She held her arm; shreds of her jacket were mixed with rags of flesh. Her face was smeared with blood.

Sarah Lee knelt down beside Johnny. His shoulder was smashed and useless; dark blood soaked through his jacket. She wiped the mud off his face with her sleeve; his eyes were closed and each breath he took was shallow. She talked to him. She told him things to comfort him; she asked him questions and gave him time to reply. When he did not, she smoothed his hair and straightened creases from his shirt.

Anger flared in Hackett at the sight of his daughter stooped over Johnny.

'Get away from him,' Hackett barked. 'He ain't nothing to do with you.'

Sarah Lee straightened Johnny's clothes as best she could. She went back to cleaning the blood off his face. Even though Hackett was only a few feet away she was so absorbed in what she was doing that she didn't hear him shouting at her to stop.

Sarah Lee didn't stop. She didn't look up. She seemed to have forgotten where she was and that there was anyone else there. She was alone with Johnny, who was hurt too badly to open his eyes and whose blood was soaking through his clothes.

Clem stepped off the last of the porch steps into the mud; his .45 was levelled at Hackett.

'I'm taking you in.'

Hackett turned towards him.

'What?'

'Take your gun out of its holster real slow and throw it down.'

Clem's words didn't make sense; Hackett stared. He turned towards the saloon porch and looked for an explanation from Clem's pa, but he had ducked back inside.

'Now,' Clem said.

'What nonsense is this?' Hackett said.

'Attempted murder, theft, cover-up,' Clem said. 'Any judge will put you in jail.'

'You ain't a Pinkerton. You ain't even a deputy. What do you mean, *taking me in?*'

'I mean what I say,' Clem said.

He thumbed back the hammer of his .45.

'You walked out on this place. You walked out on the Pinkertons,' Hackett sneered. 'What are you trying to pull?'

'Throw down your weapon,' Clem said. 'I'm gonna lock you in the jailhouse.'

'My jail?' Hackett roared.

Clem's pa barged through the saloon door He held a fistful of shotgun cartridges in one hand and the gun in the other. Clem hardly noticed.

Kneeling in the mud, Sarah Lee cradled Johnny's head with her good arm and stared at him. Johnny looked up at her, his face painted white with pain.

'I ain't gonna tell you again.' Clem's words were clear and hard like glass.

A sneer turned the corners of Hackett's mouth. Clem expected Hackett to draw on him and watched for the slightest movement, anything that might give his intentions away.

In the same moment as they heard Clem's pa pull

back the twin hammers of the shotgun a pistol shot echoed between the buildings. Sarah Lee held Johnny's .45. The shotgun Clem's pa had levelled at Clem jerked up into the air; the twin barrels punched a hole in the porch roof. His huge body crashed down and the shotgun was flung aside.

'He went back inside for more shells,' Sarah Lee screamed.

Hackett dashed past her and clambered onto the porch to where Clem's pa's body was awkwardly splayed. Red veins laced across his purple cheeks; his eyes were wide with surprise; a patch of dark blood spread across his chest. The shotgun lay a couple of yards away. Hackett reached down to feel for a pulse.

'He was aiming right at you.' Sarah Lee looked at Clem. Her voice cracked.

'She's right,' Johnny said. 'He was going to fire.' His words were barely a whisper.

Sarah Lee stared down at the gun that she still held in her hand.

'Enough,' Hackett yelled.

He stormed down the porch steps, strode over to where Sarah Lee knelt on the ground. He made a grab for her; at the same time he kicked at Johnny, who cried out as his broken bones shifted together. With one arm Hackett tried to wrestle Sarah Lee to her feet, with his other hand he went for his gun.

Clem fired then. Hackett fell backwards into the mud.

As the echo of the shot died, no one spoke. No one moved.

Johnny fought to stay conscious above the pain. Sarah Lee stared at the Colt in her hand as if it was some alien thing and she was struggling to understand what it was doing there. Clem slipped his gun back into its holster.

Sarah Lee laid the pistol down beside her and turned back to Johnny. She slipped an arm under him and started to help him up. Clem crossed over to her and between them they eased him on to his feet.

As they helped him up the porch steps, they noticed Pa Passmore outside his store, staring down the street towards them.

Inside the saloon Sarah Lee gathered up cushions and made a bed for Johnny on the floor next to the stove. She held a cup of water to his lips and encouraged him to drink. When this exhausted him, she let him lie back and close his eyes.

Clem stoked the fire until the room was warm again. He and Sarah Lee sat silently on saloon chairs beside the makeshift bed, each of them lost in a mist of their own thoughts.

Images filled Clem's head of the town street as it had been when he was a kid, when it ran as far as the horizon and stretched as wide as the prairie. He remembered the people coming and going – giants most of them, all intent on serious business, who stopped only to hold important conversations. He remembered Sarah Lee peeping at him from behind her ma's skirts; he remembered the thrill of excitement that passed through him when Passmore opened the glass candy jar that stood on the counter of the store.

Sarah Lee went to wash the blood off her face and came back holding ice wrapped in a cloth. A purple bruise blossomed over the bridge of her nose.

'When he wakes we'll get that shoulder strapped up,' she said. 'Doc Hanson will be in town in an hour.'

Turning her chair to the window, Sarah Lee watched the morning light outside.

With her back to him so that Clem couldn't see her battered face, he could imagine that none of this had happened. It could be that he had merely returned home and there was Sarah Lee grown up. In the long years he had been away, he had thought of her some-times. He had imagined her as some rancher's wife with a brood of children, living a life of early mornings and sunny afternoons. He had thought of Johnny as a businessman, with the brains to expand the farm and make a successful life for himself.

That it had not turned out like this both surprised Clem and did not surprise him. While he had been away he had forced himself to think only good things of his home town, rosy thoughts to comfort himself during the lonely nights. All the rest of it he pushed to the back of his mind: his pa's drunkenness, Hackett's arrogance, Johnny's cleverness which got him nowhere.

Hackett was still spread eagled in the street; Clem's pa was sprawled across the porch. Someone would have to ask Passmore to bring the funeral cart, Clem reflected.

Clem had seen so much death. He witnessed the

killing fields during the war. Then afterwards, chasing outlaws for the agency, he saw innocent lives lost, bystanders killed by chance. Hackett and his pa were one more corrupt sheriff and one more drunken bully. They pleaded kin and local loyalty; Clem knew them for what they were.

Outside, the clouds cleared and sunlight filled the windows of the saloon. Sarah Lee sat and watched the sky. Johnny's eyes were closed; his breathing was regular and quick. As Clem put another log on the stove, he heard running feet clatter up the porch steps. The door burst open. Passmore leaned in the doorway, breathless from having dashed up the street.

'Came out earlier on when I heard the shooting,' he gasped. 'Thought you were all dead. No one will come down here. Got a whole crowd of people in my store.'

He looked around, took in Sarah Lee with her broken face and Johnny, ash pale, lying by the stove. He muttered something about Doc Hanson being in town soon.

Sarah Lee started to explain but Passmore got lost in the details.

'I'm just glad you're all right,' he interrupted her. 'But that ain't why I've come down here. Now I know Clem's alive, I got something to tell him.'

15

'Jesse James was in my store.'

Passmore beamed, certain that celebrity had rubbed off on him.

'Stood there bold as brass, 'bout as far from me as you are now.'

Clem closed the door to the stove and stood up.

'Knocked on the door. Said he'd seen a light. Asked me if I knew who he was,' Passmore continued. 'I said, "Yes I do. You're Jesse James the outlaw." '

Passmore shifted from foot to foot with excitement. 'Said that right to his face. You know what he did?'

Passmore waited for Clem to shake his head.

'No,' Clem said.

'Laughed,' Passmore said. 'Laughed out loud and said, "That's right".'

'Where is he now?' Clem demanded.

Passmore flapped his hand to show he was unwilling to have his story interrupted.

'Know what he wanted?'

154

'No.' Clem answered. He glanced at Sarah Lee.

'Wanted to know if there was any Pinkertons in town.'

Passmore paused.

'Know what I told him?'

'Just tell us,' Clem said.

'No there ain't,' Passmore said. 'There was three of 'em but they rode out.'

Passmore grinned at his own cleverness. 'I watched 'em leave at first light and I didn't want Jesse James to catch me in a lie.'

'Didn't tell him about me?' Clem said.

'Why should I?' Passmore grinned. 'You ain't a Pinkerton no more.'

'Where is he now?' Clem said.

Passmore ignored him. 'Asked me for a sack of Bull Durham. Paid for it and told me to keep the change.' Passmore opened his hand and held out a silver dollar. 'See?' He laughed delightedly.

'After that we heard shooting. He sent me out into the street to take a look.'

'He was in the store?' Clem said.

'Had a gun on me all the while. I went back in and told him it was some dispute between the sheriff and one of the farmers he plays poker with. After that, he made me put out the oil lamps.'

Passmore looked from Clem to Sarah Lee to make sure they were following.

'Made me wait with him till everything had gone quiet,' Passmore said. 'Then he rode out.'

'Which way?' Clem snapped.

'Opposite way to the Pinkertons.'

Clem moved towards the door.

'That was an hour ago,' Passmore said. 'Told me to wait an hour before I said anything. Said if anyone came after him sooner than that, he'd know it was me who told 'em.'

The old man shuddered.

'Said he'd be watching to see if anyone came after him,' Passmore went on. 'Don't you even think about following him. No reward ain't worth a bullet.'

Passmore helped Sarah Lee down to the store where one of the townswomen would attend to her bruises. She was weak with shock, and leaned on his arm. Clem waited with Johnny until Doc Hanson arrived.

Hanson set Johnny's shoulder in a splint and arranged that he should stay in the room behind the store, where someone could keep an eye on him.

With Johnny and Sarah Lee being looked after, Clem rode out of town after the Pinkertons. Hours later he was able to tell them the direction Jesse James was headed. He accompanied them back to town but, in spite of Jackson's insistence, wouldn't ride with them any further.

Sunlight was failing by the time Clem turned his horse towards his pa's place. When he left town he was undecided what to do next but as soon as he saw the old, run-down farm, he knew.

Clem walked round the neglected buildings in the failing light. He noted the ruined fences, the chicken coops that foxes had broken open, the empty barn that had once been piled with hay. A sour whiskey smell seeped from the still.

Clem gathered the remains of straw from the corners of the barn and made a heap against the windward side of a wall. He gathered sticks, old broken fence posts, anything dry enough and piled them on the straw. When there was enough to make a blaze, he took out his flint. The straw caught easily; Clem found an old oil lamp and doused the wood.

Yellow flames licked the walls. Draught from between the barn's cottonwood planking encouraged the flames to run up to the rafters. As they burned through, tinder-dry joists crashed down onto the still. Before the whole roof caught, parts of the wall crashed in and the barn was ablaze.

The barn was a tower of flame against the night sky. The crackle and spit of the burning wood was interrupted by explosions of breaking glass from the bottles stacked inside.

After leading his horse a safe distance away and tethering him to a broken gatepost, Clem returned to the blaze. On his way across the yard he upended the old chicken coops and lobbed them into the inferno. What was to be gained by leaving the cabin? He approached the blaze, arm raised to shield himself from the wall of heat, and started to pull timbers out of the fire. He carried them over to the cabin and threw them in through the open door. The furniture went up like matchwood before a long flame bit into the wooden walls.

Content that within an hour or two there would be

157

nothing left, Clem mounted up and headed back into town. He would bed down in the livery stable, catch a few hours' sleep and ride out in the morning. If things hadn't gone awry at Kearney, he never would have taken the hometown trail. He had never intended to stay.

The following morning, Passmore was behind the counter in the store as usual. A crowd of customers pressed close to get a good view of the silver dollar he held out in his hand. He had already told the story twice from start to finish that morning; if another audience presented itself, he would tell it again.

Sarah Lee was sitting with Johnny in the storeroom out back where Passmore had made him up a makeshift bed. Johnny was pale, bright-eyed and his skin glistened like wax. Sarah Lee held a mug of herbal tea to his lips. Lying back against Ma Passmore's old quilt, the slightest movement caused him agony.

They both smiled to see Clem. Johnny's voice was weak and the effort of talking was too much. Sarah Lee said that they both had to concentrate on recovery; in a few weeks they would be able to sort out a new life for themselves. Both of them knew about the fire; it had been the talk of the store that morning. The flames were visible for miles. The townsfolk had assumed there had been some accident with the still, but Sarah Lee guessed different.

'And the cabin?' Sarah Lee said.

'Everything,' Clem said.

'You ain't staying?' There was sadness in Sarah Lee's voice but she was resigned.

'I'll ride after the Pinkertons,' Clem said. 'Jackson wanted me to pin on my badge again.'

'Rejoin them?'

'They're on the trail of Jesse James. I want to be there if they catch him.'

Sarah Lee got to her feet and held Clem for a moment.

'Don't say goodbye,' she said.

She pulled away from him.

'I'll ride out to your place now and again.' She looked down at Johnny. 'We both will, just to look over it for you.'

'Use the grazing for your horses,' Clem said. 'Can't say when I'll be back.'

Sarah Lee parcelled up some of Passmore's hard tack and filled Clem's canteen for him. Standing in the doorway to the store, she watched him head out. He was less than a day's ride behind the Pinks. The morning light was bright and the frozen ground made the going good.

At the edge of town Clem reined in his horse. He slipped the Pinkerton badge from his pocket and pinned it to his jacket where he had worn it before. He turned in the saddle and waved an arc in the sky back in the direction of the store. He was far away now. From this distance, he could hardly tell the store apart from any of the other buildings. He shaded his eyes but still couldn't see. More than that he couldn't say for sure whether there was a figure in the doorway who waved back, but something told him there was.